Divorc ... *...eeps*
on giving!

CLASSIFIED AD: For sale. Wedding dress. Worn once—by mistake.

"Another one of our many disagreements. He wants a no-fault divorce, whereas I would prefer to have the bastard crucified."

"Divorce: the end of an error..."

"An open marriage is nature's way of telling you that you need a divorce."

"I married Mr. Right. I just didn't know his middle name was Always."

"Love is the quest! Marriage, the conquest! Divorce, the inquest!"

Can I Kill Him Now?

Kathleen Hering

Kathleen Hering

Published August 2018
By Kathleen Hering
Albany, Oregon

.

ISBN13: 978-1718655171
ISBN-10: 1718655177

"A good friend will help you move. A best friend will help you move a dead body."

1

This was humiliating.

Ellie was left to clean up after her husband again. This time while the neighborhood wives watched from the front windows of their cookie cutter homes...

She caught the women across the street peering out between their made-to-order drapery panels while their husbands jogged out to the curbside mailboxes two hours before the mailman—er, mailperson—was due to arrive. Each of the men (and the one "domestic partner") looked toward Ellie's driveway, gathering information to report back to his spouse.

Jake from the moving company had pounded on Ellie's front door just before noon, waving a clipboard with a pink sheet of paper authorizing him to load and haul her former husband's belongings. The bright orange truck filled the entire driveway slab, hiding the hand-cut stone squares her husband had insisted on having installed when they contracted to have their house built. ("Model 3B, Section 2, Skyview subdivision. Driveway add-on extra.")

Last night Ellie had used over-sized, bright yellow post-it notes to tag any furniture that was supposed to go in the mammoth truck. She wanted to avoid having to say good-bye to some of her favorite pieces in front of the moving crew today.

"Who cries over an antique leather trunk?" she asked herself last night.

"Apparently, I do," she'd answered and reached for a Kleenex and two chocolate chip cookies to fortify her while she wandered through the rooms with a pen in one hand and the gummed yellow notes and the cookies balanced in the other.

This afternoon she was straining to be cordial to the movers. It wasn't their fault that her ex-husband was a jerk.

"How many driving days are there between here and Colorado?" she asked the van driver. He seemed to be in charge of Operation Outta Here.

"Without federal regulations, we could probably do it in two days," Jake said. "As it is, we've notified your husband…"

"Ex-husband," she said.

"Right. We've notified Mr. Mobley to expect us on the 15th of the month."

"And, you're sure everything is safe and secure and that no one will open the truck between here and Colorado? The stuff doesn't get stored in a warehouse somewhere?" she asked.

"Absolutely sure. 'Direct transport.'"

"And my husband's paying for all this?"

Ex-husband, he thought, but he didn't correct her. He nodded.

"I'm curious," she said. "How much does a move like this cost?"

"Don't know yet, ma'am. The company charges by the pound."

Ellie turned to walk away, then stopped short. "Did you just say 'by the *pound*?'" she asked.

"Yep."

"Oh, darn!" she said. "I forgot some things. Clarke would kill me if I kept them. He'd think I did it on purpose. Tell me you have space for three small items."

"What?" Jake asked as he continued locking the back of the van.

"Well, two medium-sized things and one not-so-large box. It'll just take me a minute to find them, and it'll spare me having to deal with Clarke Mobley again."

Jake sighed and reached toward the sliding security bar and chain lock on the back of the truck. He lifted the

3

metal bar and unlocked the doors while Ellie ran back into the house.

Ellie's earlier "special packing" effort had gone undetected today. Now she needed to add the final touch. Neither Jake nor his two college-age assistants had noticed her earlier sabotage when they loaded the dark brown leather recliner. The over-sized chair that still had the indentation of Clarke Mobley's sorry backside on the cushion...

She had heard of women vandalizing their ex-husband's belongings or hiding a few raw fish in a box of clothing, but that seemed so vindictive. She could never stoop to that level, she thought. Instead, Ellie removed the gold foil wrappers from half a dozen hand-dipped dark-chocolate-covered cherry candies and tucked the confections neatly between the plush folds in the reclining chair's upholstery. She'd added two of the gold wrappers for effect. She wanted to make sure Clarke understood the gesture. It seemed appropriate. The receipt she'd found from "Ye Olde Sweet Shoppe" had been her first clue that Clarke had purchased candy for someone other than her.

"Eager to help," Ellie had said earlier this morning as she held the door open while it took three men to lift the heavy recliner out to the moving truck. She remembered that yesterday's online issue of The Oregonian newspaper reported that ski lodges in Colorado were struggling to make a profit since unseasonably warm weather had swept across the state. *That locked moving van could get plenty hot,* she thought.

4

Now, she circled the inside of the attached garage. She quickly collected the items that would complete the load in the van.

She maneuvered the heavy-weight U-Haul dolly back to the driveway. A large corrugated cardboard box marked "Encyclopedia Britannica—complete set" was first. She sat on the garage floor and used her feet to help push the box onto the steel platform on the dolly. Two heavy fireplace andirons were balanced on top of the box of books.

"While your guys load these things," she told Jake, "maybe you can help me get the weight set out to the truck. It will mean so much to Clarke."

"Whatever you say," he said. "You know we move canned goods," he offered. "One woman sent the piano."

"Oh?"

"When I asked if her ex played, she said 'just the ponies.'" He chuckled at his own story.

Ellie hesitated, did a half turn, and looked over her shoulder at the hand cart.

"No canned goods," she said, "but Clarke can have that heavy dolly."

THE NEXT MORNING at 8:17 (the digital clock stayed) someone pounded on Ellie's front door.

"What the heck is that?" she asked the cat. *It couldn't be the moving guys returning,* she thought. She gently pushed the cat off the bed and threw on a terrycloth bathrobe, tying the thick sash as she walked to the front door. "Who is it?" she called through the door.

"That's what effen' peepholes are for," yelled a familiar voice.

"Watch your mouth. The cat's awake," came Ellie's response. She opened the door and saw her friend Trish, who held a tray of home-baked cinnamon buns. Trish reached inside to give Ellie a one-armed hug.

"Sorry about the noise. I was trying to sound like a man. A big man. Hell, a hit man."

"And that would be *why*?" Ellie asked.

"In case Clarke's here," Trish whispered.

"Clarke's long gone. So come on in—and bring your friends," Ellie said as she reached for the tray.

Trish took half a dozen steps inside. She stopped, swiveled in place, and looked from wall to wall in the living room.

"The place looks empty," she said.

"Half empty," Ellie corrected. "Clarke's stuff left in a moving van late yesterday."

"Why didn't you call me?"

Ellie shrugged and dug in her robe pocket for a used Kleenex.

"I've got it!" Trish shouted. "That hunkin' recliner's gone. I'd have taken a chainsaw and cut that sucker down the middle."

"Clarke got the chainsaw. Cup of coffee?"

"He left the coffeemaker?" Trish asked. "That was generous of the Shit."

"Watch your mouth. I got the cat."

"The cat you both hate?" Trish asked.

"I've warmed to Felix lately."

"Only because you know if you catch him catting around, he won't take the good silverware as he leaves."

"The coffee's instant," Ellie said, handing her friend an ugly stoneware mug Clarke had rejected. "I don't cook in my new life."

"Is there a reason the china cabinet is empty?" Trish asked. "Wait. Don't tell me."

"He got the wedding china. It's just as well. I was having late night visions of throwing it at him—piece by piece."

"He's planning a formal dinner for sixteen?" Trish asked.

"Clarke doesn't know a tureen from a teapot."

"So," Trish said brightly. "What are you going to do now?"

"First, add a shot of something to this instant coffee," Ellic said.

"The man left the liquor?"

"Oh, hell."

2

"What? No moving van?"

"You thought it was coming back?" Ellie asked when Trish arrived on the front porch the second morning in a row. "The moving guys left for Fantasyland and should be halfway to Colorado by now."

"I thought it would take them a couple of days to load up," Trish said. "They must know their stuff."

"Speaking of stuff, I have a confession to make," Ellie said.

"I hope this is good." Trish helped herself to a lukewarm cup of tea from the art deco look-alike teapot on her friend's kitchen counter.

"Depends on your point of view. Remember when I told you about planting the candy in the recliner?"

9

"Yeah! A second high-five to you, girl."

Ellie didn't raise her hand.

"I didn't tell you the complete story," she said. "Before the van left, I climbed back in and took the candy out of the recliner."

"You didn't," Trish said.

"Afraid so. But I left the wrappers."

"You wimp!"

"I kept thinking I was above all that. And, in the end, I was."

"Boo hiss," Trish said. "We've been friends all these years. Have I taught you nothing?"

"Why should I take out my anger on a chair? I know what Clarke and I paid for that stupid recliner. Besides, he'll get the message when he finds the wrappers."

"And that message would be?"

"That I'm a wimp?" Ellie asked.

"Bingo!" Trish put her arm around her friend. "No." she said. "He'll remember he had the best woman on Earth. And now he's got Bimbo the Slut who would have sliced that leather upholstery to pieces with the heel of a stiletto."

"One can only hope."

"The sun's trying to come out. Why don't we move out to the back deck?" Trish suggested. "This place depresses me."

"You'll be more depressed when you see the deck."

"He took that too?"

"No," Ellie said. "But I had to put all the new deck furniture and outdoor umbrella on his side of the list."

"I thought you bought those things with the money you inherited from your mom's estate."

"It's called 'community property,'" Ellie explained.

"Well, I say we drive to some Colorado community and take it back."

It was the first Ellie had smiled today. No, she wasn't going to steal the expensive teak furniture, but knowing that Trish would have done it for her made her feel good. She wasn't alone.

Trish was the Thelma to her latent Louise. The Lucy to her Ethel... The Rhoda to her Mary...

"So, if we aren't going to soak in the limited Oregon sunshine to get more age spots, what do you suggest?"

"I'm thinking, now that most of the big pieces are gone, I ought to rearrange the furniture," Ellie said. "Maybe go for the minimalist look."

"I thought you were selling the place."

"I am, but I have to live somewhere until then."

"You could move in with Harvey and me," Trish suggested.

"Thanks, but no thanks. That signals 'needy.'" A single tear threatened in the corner of Ellie's left eye.

"No tears today!" Trish commanded.

"I had a mental flash of Clarke skiing with that woman."

"Screw the bastard," Trish said.

And, that became Ellie's silent mantra. She couldn't say those words aloud, for fear the nuns at Saint Mark's parochial school would come back from the dead and reach for their rulers. But she could darn well think them.

INSOMNIA WAS NEW to Ellie and she wasn't happy about it. This was the third morning she had been awake at 3 a.m., surprised that she was alone in the house. She decided to make good use of her time and got up out of bed and posed in front of the bathroom mirror to trim her bangs.

"Of course, you're alone," she chided herself. "Clarke took a powder and Antonia is safe in her dorm room at Portland State."

Antonia. Their daughter's name had been Clarke's idea. He was in his Renaissance Italian period when the baby was due. They'd been too broke to replace the roof of their first home with the old-world Italian tiles Clarke wanted. Instead, he inflicted his interest in Italy on their unborn child. Like so many other times, Ellie had yielded to his choice. She later thanked the fertility gods that she hadn't delivered a son named Gugliano Vicenzio. It would have taken the boy his entire kindergarten year to learn to write his name. Any idiot knows the luckiest kids in beginning penmanship classes are named Ann Lee or Joe Jones.

It had sounded so rational when she and Clarke talked about making sure they didn't force their daughter to take sides during the divorce. Very adult.

12

"Very dumb," Ellie said aloud as the cat stretched on the sheets beside her. Ellie missed Antonia—now Toni, which fit better on a cheerleading megaphone. The college campus was less than two hours from home, but that didn't stop Ellie from missing her only child.

Clarke had promised to travel from Colorado to Oregon later in the month to visit Toni. And Toni had promised to alert her mom to the date of his visit so Ellie could decide if she wanted to see the man. Not.

It had been considerate of Clarke to wait for his midlife crisis until Toni was old enough that child support wasn't an issue, Ellie thought with her tongue planted firmly against the inside of her right cheek.

All very civilized. All tremendously modern. All incredibly stupid.

3

"I still don't understand why you have to sell the house," Trish said. "Says who?"

"Well, Clarke, for one."

"You don't have to do what Clarke says. It's called *divorce*."

"It's part of the divorce decree," Ellie said. "To keep the business, I have to pay Clarke the equity we have in the house. Or sell the house and split what's left after escrow closes."

"January isn't a red-hot real estate month," Trish pointed out.

"Tell me about it. Business at the garden center has tanked, but it always does this month. Then it blossoms again right before Easter."

"Cute."

"That's why we push every live Christmas tree, door swag and evergreen wreath we can during December," Ellie explained. "We had good sales during November and December this past year. I should be able to make it through January and February. We have a skeleton staff for those two months, and I left Santos manning the store."

"I don't understand. How was the division of property decided?" Trish asked.

"Clarke and I and our attorneys sat down with an arbitrator."

"Was Bambi Maguire there?" asked Trish, breaking with her vow not to utter the *other* woman's name.

"She would have been, but my attorney objected."

"I should think so," Trish said indignantly.

"But, it didn't matter," Ellie continued. "Clarke hired Bambi's attorney sister to represent him during the divorce proceedings."

"He what?"

"I kid you not. He hired Bunny Maguire."

"She's cutthroat. I've heard stories about her for years," Trish said. "She has her own law firm."

"My attorney told me other lawyers in town refer to Bambi and her counselor sister as 'the Fauna Fam,'" Ellie said. "A judge slipped once and called Bunny 'Counselor Fauna.' As the story goes, the judge was threatened with a written reprimand."

"Who would name their daughters Bunny and Bambi?"

"Careful. I could have had a son called Gugliani," Ellie said. "'Google' for short on the soccer roster."

"How soon do you have to sell the house?" Trish asked, guiding the conversation back toward the current situation.

"I have until June 30th. If the local real estate market isn't moving..."

"And, it's not," Trish said.

"...I can drop the price some or refinance the garden center to make up the difference. But, that would be a last resort."

"Says who?"

"Says the divorce documents we both signed."

"And what's in it for you?" Trish asked.

"Half the joint property, like I said. The better car..."

"That I recall you bought from your inheritance check. But I repeat myself."

"True," Ellie said. "And half the savings, which, by the time I caught on to Clarke's affair, was below forty-five thousand dollars."

"Stocks? Bonds?"

"They were in Clarke's name and he'd sold them— quite by coincidence—six months earlier. He claimed the profit went into running 'the marital household.'"

"Unbelievable!" Trish looked around at the furnishings that were left in the living room.

"Don't go there," Ellie said. "I've gotten past that."

17

"You're right! Absolutely! You're going to have a wonderful new life."

"Do you truly believe that?" Ellie asked.

"Work with me here."

THE NEWSPAPER CLIPPING arrived by mail the next day. It was in a hand-addressed envelope with a floral U.S. postage stamp. Ellie didn't recognize the handwriting on the envelope, and there was no return address. At first, it was a relief to find something other than a past-due bill in her mailbox.

She tore open the envelope and a clipped news article that was tucked inside fluttered to the floor. She bent down to pick it up.

There was a photo with the news story, displayed under the headline "Wedding Bells." The photo showed Clarke Mobley and Bambi Maguire, wearing smiles that would have made an orthodontist proud.

Except to note that her ex-husband was wearing a new suit, Ellie told herself that she wasn't interested in the article. The depth of her loss re-surfaced, though, when she skimmed the story and read that the new Mr. and Mrs. Mobley were taking a honeymoon cruise before returning to their first home. The writer stopped short of providing an address for said home or Ellie would have resealed the envelope and printed *RETURN TO SENDER* on the outside.

She picked up the cat and sat down on the loveseat. "I can take it," she told Felix and read aloud:

"The couple is making their first home in Aspen, where they have purchased commercial property to open a recreational and medical marijuana dispensary." Ellie had heard from Antonia that Clarke planned to open the dispensary, but she'd hoped he was kidding. Apparently that report was true.

Ellie glanced again at the photo. Clarke looked tired standing next to the young Bambi who was draped in soft layers of flowing organza that created the illusion of Woodstock—the Sequel.

"The bride works part-time at Nail It Salon," she continued. Ellie doubted that Felix could tell that she was now making up the words. "The bride wore an antique lace veil, held in place by feathered roach clips," she finished.

Ellie put the article on the kitchen table in case Trish wanted to read the actual words later. *That's what good friends were for*, she thought. To cry at your wedding—and torch the news article about your ex-spouse's next wedding

4

Ellie's list of reasons to resent her ex-husband grew daily. *It might be time to get a spiral notebook*, she thought. *College-ruled.*

She resented that Clarke had never liked her friend Trish. Ellie had quizzed him about that once, and Clarke had mumbled something about the two women being total opposites—and returned to watching ESPN.

His assessment of Trish was probably one of the few honest things he'd said to Ellie in the year before he filed for divorce.

She and Trish *were* opposites. That's why the friendship worked, Ellie had explained to the man who never listened.

Clarke Mobley didn't understand why Ellie chose Trish. There were just shy of four million residents in Oregon, and his wife had chosen Trish Grover. The woman was nothing like Ellie. Clarke could tick off their differences on one hand:

Ellie was the quieter of the two. And, well, proper. Trish Grover grew louder and border-line vulgar after a couple of beers at their neighborhood picnics.

His wife Ellie dressed conservatively. Trish favored plunging necklines and had the cleavage to do them justice.

Ellie was taller and thinner and wore jeans and sweatshirts during the workday at the garden shop. Her friend was shorter and chose bright-colored clothes that drew men's attention. When Trish was hired at a clothing boutique downtown, her husband Harvey joked that Trish spent her weekly paycheck before she left her job each Friday.

Ellie refused to bleach her light-brown hair to please Clarke. He told Ellie once that Trish's long, blonde hair was the woman's only redeeming quality.

The two couples moved to the neighborhood the same summer. Within a week, both wives received hand-written invitations from the owner of the two-story house on the corner.

Welcome to the Neighborhood!

Please join us Friday at 7 p.m. for Bunco.

Cecelia and Catherine

AFTER THE SECOND round of Bunco, Trish and Ellie exchanged glances over the game table. It was obvious that the "regulars" took their Bunco seriously.

22

Who cared if one of the women had inflated her score? Ellie coughed to disguise her surprise when the angry voices rose at the table. It probably wasn't good Bunco etiquette to laugh, she thought.

"I'm going to get Ellie some water," Trish told their hostess. She grabbed Ellie by the hand and they slipped past the sink and out the kitchen door without a word to each other.

"So many 'Babies,' so many 'Buncos,'" Trish said as they made their escape across the yard. "I've got a bottle of white wine at my place," she added.

Ten minutes later, they were perched on the stools at the counter in Trish's kitchen talking non-stop. They switched from wine to Diet Pepsi after the first round of drinks.

By 10 p.m., Ellie had decided that Clarke might miss her—those were the days—and headed across the street and up the block to her own house where she found Clarke asleep in front of the television. Evidently he hadn't missed her after all.

Ellie and Trish still used "Bunco" as their code word for an awkward situation. When they had waited over twenty minutes for service at a restaurant last week, it had been Trish who suggested that the two of them "Bunco on out of here."

5

Ellie stirred in her chair when she heard a phone ringing in the distance. When it continued to ring, she woke from an impromptu nap and answered the phone.

"Were you outside, Mom?"

"Toni. I didn't expect to hear from you during exam week."

"The R.A. said I should call you. So here I am."

"R.A.?" Ellie asked.

"Residence Advisor, Mom. Remember the guy you met when we checked in at the dorm in September?"

Ellie remembered him. He looked the same age as the incoming freshmen, but he spoke like an adult. "Yes, ma'am. No, ma'am. Call me any time, sir."

"The police were here today and wanted to talk to me about Dad. Brad said they couldn't talk to me without a lawyer present. The cops said they could because I'm over 18. And Brad told them to come back in an hour."

"Brad?"

"The R.A., Mom. Weren't you listening?"

"Let's slow this down," Ellie said. "Are you OK?"

"Of course. Why wouldn't I be?"

"When the police returned, what did they say to you?"

"Brad wouldn't let them talk to me until the legal counsel on campus could sit in on the conversation," Toni repeated.

"Smart man, your Brad," Ellie said.

"The police finally talked to me and the lawyer dude. They wanted to know if I knew where Dad is."

"And you said?"

"I told them that, as far as I knew, he was in Colorado with Thumper."

"Toni, be respectful," Ellie said. "It's Bambi."

"One in the same to me," Toni said. "So anyway, they wanted to know the last time I had seen Dad and if I had talked to him by phone or had an email from him in the past two weeks."

Ellie rubbed her hand across her forehead. She thought she'd done such a good job raising Antonia, but it was now obvious that she had never stressed to her daughter the importance of getting directly to the point in conversation.

"And you told them?" she prompted.

"I told them that the last time I saw him was when he flew out of PDX to Denver. I gave him a ride to the airport."

"Did the police give you any idea why they were asking about your dad?" This was a conversation Ellie never thought she'd be having with her daughter. Clarke may have forgotten his original wedding vows, but he'd never done anything illegal. As far as she knew...

"No. And, when I asked them, the older cop said, 'We ask the questions.' Real snotty like."

"Did they mention your dad's new wife?"

"No."

"What else did they ask?"

"Just the usual kind of stuff. Except they wanted to know how long you guys had lived in our house and if you had a vacation home or any place else you stayed."

If only, Ellie thought. If so, she'd drive to campus, pick up Toni, and escape from all the madness for a week at the imaginary cedar-lined cabin near Crater Lake.

"I'm glad you called me. You sure you're OK?"

"Of course. Oh, and Mom? They didn't exactly say so, but I got the idea that maybe Bambi had reported Dad missing."

"I don't think so, honey. Somebody mailed me their wedding announcement last week. It had to be either Bambi or your dad."

"Great! Well, I've gotta go. I've got class in ten minutes."

Ellie put her not-so-smart phone down on the counter. It had taken her weeks to learn to maneuver icons on the phone's black plastic screen. She also disliked that she could be reached at any minute of the day or night now. And, since that was the case, why hadn't the police contacted *her* if they had questions about the whereabouts of her ex-husband? Why upset their daughter?

The problem with divorce, she thought, was that you may have gotten rid of a cheating spouse, but you still shared your memories and a child.

ELLIE INCHED THE CAR into the garage. It was easier to unpack the grocery bags from there and enter through the laundry room. She closed the overhead garage door and stepped past the car with the first two brown paper bags in her arms.

"Save a tree by using plastic?" she said to Felix who greeted her. "Or, spoil the environment with errant plastic bags?" she pondered aloud.

Felix didn't appear to have the answer either.

When she had four bags lined up on the kitchen counter, she picked up the cat and sat down in the living room to catch her breath.

"I know," she told the cat. "It'll take us two weeks to eat all that. But, I can't get used to shopping for one. Well, one and a loyal cat," she added.

The cat didn't seem to care one way or the other about the conversation.

"You could express a little interest," Ellie told him. "You know I defended you and your fellow felines to Trish the other day."

The cat closed his eyes and tucked his head under Ellie's arm.

"Don't you even want to hear what our friend Trish said?"

No response from the cat.

Felix jumped to the floor, leaving Ellie to unpack the groceries. Ellie wondered vaguely when she had started to hate grocery shopping. Was it because cooking for one wasn't any fun? Or, was it because she dreaded passing one of her neighbors in the aisles of the grocery store.

Trish reminded her daily that it was Clarke who needed to be embarrassed, not her. But, Ellie kept thinking that there must have been something she could have done differently when she and Clarke were married.

ELLIE LATER QUESTIONED why she had been surprised to find two police officers standing at her front door the next morning. After talking to Toni, she should have expected them. The older officer took the lead and introduced himself and his partner. The younger man looked the same age as Toni.

"Could we come in?" he asked.

Both men fumbled for ID cards and flashed them toward her.

"Yes. Yes, of course. Come in. What is this about?"

"We need to ask you some questions about your ex-husband. Mrs. Mobley has reported him missing."

"No, I didn't..." Ellie stopped herself mid-sentence when she remembered that she wasn't the only "Mrs. Mobley" now.

"You have the right to have an attorney present before answering any questions," the younger cop recited. "If you cannot afford an attorney, one will be appointed for you..."

Ellie studied the two men. They were only doing their jobs, she thought. Why did she feel threatened?

"I'll call my attorney," she said, wondering if that made her look guilty of whatever the officers were investigating.

"That may be difficult," the younger man said. "This is a Saturday. If you can't reach legal counsel, please call this phone number," he said and handed her a business card from Legal Aid Society. "Someone mans the phone twenty-four hours a day, seven days a week."

"Since you opted to have an attorney present," the other officer said, "we need to schedule a time that you and your attorney can meet us at the Police Department. We're available at 10 a.m. Tuesday. Come to the front desk and someone will direct you to the right location."

"And do bring that attorney," the rookie cop said. "The case number is on the business card I handed you."

Apparently, it didn't matter if the appointment time was convenient for her, Ellie thought. She pocketed the card.

She was dialing Trish before the police car had pulled away from the curb.

"Be right there. I'll bring the wine."

"Way too early for wine," Ellie said.

"Depends. Are we toasting Clarke's possible demise or fortifying you to face a police interrogation?"

"Don't even joke about it. You can help me find the home phone number for my divorce attorney. I didn't think I'd need it again."

While she waited for Trish, Ellie sorted through the stack of business cards that were "filed" in an empty sugar bowl on the end of the kitchen counter.

Trish left the wine bottle at home, but she snagged a bag of Oreo cookies from the kitchen counter before she crossed the street and walked to Ellie's house.

"YOU KNOW WHAT I hate most?" Ellie asked.

"Just a wild guess," Trish said. "Clarke?"

"Well, yes. But—even more—I hate having to worry about him letting Toni down. It was bad enough dealing with that when I was married to the man. He'd be late or just not show up at all for something we'd planned, and I'd never know where he was. Now, I worry he's going to be one disappointment after another to Toni."

"She's a big girl."

"So was I," Ellie said. "And it still hurt."

Trish had been in the room for only five minutes and Ellie already felt calmer.

"Proud of you, girl," Trish said. "I'm not sure I would have thought to request a lawyer."

"You haven't been through a divorce proceeding with that shark attorney of Clarke's."

"No, but there's still time. I found a pair of Harvey's dirty boxers behind the bed this morning."

"Thank you!" Ellie said. "Could you repeat that story any time I even vaguely think I miss Clarke?"

"Will do."

"The cops reminded me to ask for an attorney," Ellie said.

"They couldn't have been that hostile."

Ellie ignored the comment. "I thought I knew my divorce attorney's number by heart, but I got a disconnect message, so maybe not," she said. "Then, I checked the phone book and punched in the numbers for two other lawyers whose names came to mind. Every attorney I called had a similar message on his phone: 'So and so will be out of the office until 10 a.m. Tuesday while attending the Oregon Bar Association annual meeting at Salishan.'"

Salishan was one of the pricier, convention centers in the state, Trish recalled. The more expensive rooms had beautiful ocean views. The only time she and Harv had stayed there, he claimed that visitors were charged "by the wave."

"I'm open to suggestions. What do I do now?" Ellie asked.

"Didn't you say the cop told you how to get a pro-bono attorney?"

"Pro-bono?" Ellie asked.

"Free. Or cheap, anyway."

"He gave me this business card from Legal Aid. I know the divorce was harsh, but am I entitled to a free attorney?"

"Dial the number," Trish said.

Ellie set the phone down five minutes later. "An attorney will meet me at 9 a.m. Tuesday morning at the Starbucks near the police department."

"Did they give you a name?" Trish asked.

"No. A lawyer's a lawyer at this point. I wouldn't have thought to request one if Toni hadn't called yesterday morning. The police arrived on campus to talk to her and the advisor at her dorm wouldn't let them see her 'without counsel present.'"

"That tuition money you're paying is worth every penny," Trish said.

"You don't suppose Clarke left Bambi, do you?"

"Nah," they said in unison.

AFTER HIGH SCHOOL graduation, Ellie had attended community college to be qualified as a legal assistant. Much to her parents' dismay, her education stopped there. They'd never been overly fond of Clarke and thought if he hadn't come on the scene, Ellie would have transferred to a four-year school and then gone on to law school.

Ellie was glad now that Clarke waited until after the death of her parents to show their family, friends and neighbors that he was a jerk. She suspected, though, that her father had known all along. She remembered her dad making a random remark once that having a small family might be "for the best" in case Ellie had to be the "sole breadwinner" someday.

She wished now that she had quizzed her dad. Had he been speaking from intuition or did the man know something about Clarke's character all along?

Trish, the worldlier of the two friends, had grown up in Southern California and graduated from college in Santa Barbara—where she never met a tanned, blond college man she didn't mentally rate from one to ten for future husband material.

She was as surprised as her parents when she graduated with a degree in business. She stayed on at the university and worked in the graduate admissions office, where, if she played her cards right, she could meet every male graduate student enrolling.

Harvey Grover, who was five years older than Trish, arrived to register for a two-year grad school program at the end of Trish's first year of work. She continued to work on campus a second year before she and Harv married. When they moved to Oregon, Trish decided to try the wife-at-home lifestyle for a few years before seeking employment. Both she and Harvey assumed they'd have children, but it never happened.

Harvey retired after twenty three years as a high school history teacher and an assistant principal. Both

Trish and Ellie loved to hear the stories of shenanigans pulled by kids while Harvey worked at the high school.

Their favorite tale was of the seniors who, during the week before graduation, released three goats in the main hallway at the school. As part of this senior prank, they had labeled the goats #1, #2, and #4. As Harvey told the story, high school staff members and even other students spent the better part of the school day searching for the non-existent goat #3.

Harvey missed the students since his retirement, but he didn't miss the constant supervision of night-time sporting events and away games.

TRISH HAD TO OPEN the boutique early on Tuesday morning so Ellie was on her own to meet the attorney from Legal Aid.

Ellie circled the block in her car three times before finding a parking place near Starbucks and the Police Department. She wrapped her trench coat tightly around her waist and walked the half block to Starbucks. She could hear chatter from inside the business before she opened the door.

She shuffled her way to the counter, dodging other customers so she could request a cup of regular coffee. The barista didn't hide his disappointment at not getting to concoct something more exotic. Ellie looked around the crowded room to see if she could spot anyone who looked like he might practice law.

Clarke's attorney—one of the Fauna women—was seated at a small table in a back corner near the restrooms.

"Back here," she called.

Ellie reached for a napkin to sponge up the coffee she'd splashed on the counter. The server picked up her cup and filled it to the top again. No charge.

"This is awkward," Ellie said as she crossed the room to greet the woman who had called to her. None other than Bunny Maguire, Attorney at Law.

"Not so much. It's a small town," the attorney said. "I understand that you had a house call from the police, and that they want to ask you about your former husband, Clarke Mobley."

Ellie nodded and took a tiny sip of the still-too-hot coffee. "Will going to the interview with me be a conflict of interest for you?" she asked.

"Not for me. The Mobley divorce case is closed," Ms. Maguire said. "I haven't talked to the 'happy couple' since they moved to Colorado. Have you?"

"No." The woman's reference to the "happy couple" took Ellie by surprise. She thought it was in poor taste.

Bunny's outfit had an air of sophistication that only she or Jackie O. could have pulled off. The charcoal sheath dress was topped by a calf-length textured light grey coat. Fashionably understated. Tight black leather stack-heeled boots filled the gap between the hem of the coat and the ground. Large-hooped earrings—her only jewelry—whispered "real gold, folks."

Bunny Maguire pulled a yellow legal pad from her briefcase and got down to business.

"This appointment with the boys in blue will be very brief," she said. "Listen carefully. During the interview, glance at me before you answer any question. If I look bored, go ahead and answer. If you see my lips mouthing "no," you zip yours. I'll step in and shut off that particular line of questioning. I may even be able to convince them to wait to interview you until they have confirmed that the man is actually missing. Knowing Bambi as I do..."

"OK. Is there anything else I need to know?" Ellie asked.

"No. That pretty much covers it," Ms. Maguire said. "Throw your shoulders back, look confident, and follow my lead. We should be out of there in twenty minutes tops." She hesitated. "Unless you killed the bastard and buried him in the basement."

"We don't have a basement."

6

"Your full name, birth date, and address, please."

Ellie glanced at her newly-hired attorney, who looked bored.

"My name is Elizabeth Dorothy Mobley, June 5th."

She purposely mumbled the year.

"Speak clearly, please."

"Excuse me," Attorney Maguire said. "You two were on her front porch within the past week. And names and birthdates are listed on drivers' licenses in the state of Oregon."

The cops exchanged glances and let the matter drop.

"What can you tell us about your ex-husband?"

"I'm no longer married to the man?"

Bunny Maguire smiled. "Perhaps you should tell my client what this is all about. Otherwise, I may be filing a complaint for harassment before the end of the day."

"Whoa!" the older interviewer said.

"*Never* 'whoa' me," Bunny said.

"I beg your pardon. Each of you," the officer said. "Let's start again." He cleared his throat and continued. "Mr. Mobley has been reported missing by his second wife."

"Why would that information be of interest to my client?"

"We have information that 'your client' threatened to kill her ex-husband."

"I did what?" Ellie asked.

"Did you or did you not threaten to kill Clarke Mobley?"

"Why would you think that?"

"The Judge overheard you," the man said smugly.

Ellie looked confused.

"At the end of the divorce proceedings, he heard you ask your attorney if you could 'kill him now.' And, ethically, Judge Petersen felt he needed to report that to us."

"Good grief. Is that what this is all about?" Ellie asked.

"You threatened a life," the detective said.

"I felt relief at having the man *out* of my life."

"And, I felt compelled to tell you," the detective said, "that your statement was reported to the police. Is there anything you want to tell me?"

"Absolutely not," Ellie said.

The officer addressed Ellie again. "Have you seen your ex-husband in the past month?"

"No."

Bunny kicked Ellie under the table, reminding her to glance at her attorney before answering.

"When did you last see him?"

Bunny's face was expressionless.

"At our final divorce proceedings. Going on three months now," Ellie said.

"Have you spoken to him by phone?"

Blank face.

"No," Ellie responded.

"Did you harm your husband?"

Bunny's lips looked like a platypus. Ellie guessed that signaled "Hell No."

"End of interview, gentlemen," Bunny said. She motioned Ellie to stand up.

"I beg your pardon," the second officer started.

"You can beg, steal or barter, but this interview has concluded. Please notify me directly, gentlemen, if you have substantial cause to interview my client. In other words, we are not interested in participating in a fishing expedition."

The older officer opened his mouth to speak.

"Good day, gentlemen," Bunny Maguire, Attorney at Law, said.

Ellie wasn't sure whether to speak or wave as Bunny grabbed hold of her arm and walked her out. She opted for neither.

"Let's walk around the corner to that donut shop. We can debrief while we get our sugar intake," Bunny said.

BUNNY MAGUIRE PICKED up the tab for coffees, Ellie's chocolate donut, and her own two maple bars and a cinnamon sticky bun. Ellie wondered if the woman always ate this way at morning break time or if this was also her lunch and part of dinner.

"As to our little meeting just now," Bunny started. "The officers are all bluff and no substance."

"How can you be so sure?" Ellie asked.

"That interview would been structured completely differently if they had any concrete information linking you to your husband's death. They've got one measly comment that was overheard—if we even believe that—at the end of a divorce case."

"I probably did say that," Ellie said. "I know I felt that way."

"You forget," Bunny said. "I was in that courtroom less than ten feet away from you and *I* didn't hear the remark."

Ellie exhaled deeply. Darn, this woman was good. *Perhaps I should have been the one to hire her during the divorce proceedings,* Ellie thought.

They finished their mugs of coffee and headed in different directions toward their cars. If Ellie hurried, she could get home in time to de-brief the interview with Trish.

THE MINI SUBDIVISION where Ellie and Trish lived had only sixteen homes (with vacant lots left for up to four more houses in the future.) For now, the neighbors kept the weeds down on those extra lots and some summers worked together to plant community vegetable gardens. Other years they mowed two adjoining lots for the local kids' make-shift soccer games.

The street joined one of two highways that connected the towns of Albany and Corvallis in Oregon's Willamette Valley. Had the paved street shot off the highway in the opposite direction, the street would have dead-ended at the banks of the Willamette River. Instead, the street came to an end at a farmer's fence where he grew grass seed to ship out annually. (When Ellie and Clarke moved to the area, she kept waiting patiently to see what the farmers were going to plant in all the grassy fields. Trish had explained to her gently that the grass she saw growing *was* the local crop.)

FELIX LEAPED FROM the floor to the bed thirty seconds before the alarm chirped.

"How do you *do* that?" Ellie asked the cat.

No response.

Ellie reached over and tapped the clock radio to shut off the alarm. She had run out of excuses. This was the day that she would sit down with paper and pen and work out new work schedules and job descriptions for the garden center.

She showered and dressed, then stumbled into the kitchen to cook some hot cereal in the microwave.

After one bite of the cereal, she dumped it down the garbage disposal. She was trying to eat healthy, not auditioning for sainthood.

Now sitting at the dining room table with her notebook and pen—plus a small bowl of cashews, some fresh blueberries, and a cup of tea—she tried to focus on the work schedules for the nursery. She reviewed every employee's current shift and job responsibilities. She made lists of each person's strengths and noted the assigned areas where they had worked well in the past.

She'd been at the task for twenty minutes when she stumbled across an interesting fact. Over the past six to eight months, Clarke had shifted almost every area of responsibility he used to handle to one employee or another. No wonder everyone had been run off their feet last fall, trying to greet and wait on customers while bringing in the early holiday stock. She'd been too busy to notice at the time.

Clarke hadn't re-hired for empty slots created when two young employees returned to college in September either. That would have been a way to save a little money for September through January, she thought. But now, heading into spring, there weren't enough employees to wait on customers, check incoming stock, and keep up with inventory and the orders that had to be placed. Add those tasks to monitoring the sprinkler systems, rotating the perennials to keep the terra cotta pots looking their best, and trying to keep the annuals moving from the nursery to local yards...

In past years, Clarke had done hiring in the fall so the new staff would have time to shadow another employee for a few weeks. Had Clarke simply forgotten?

And where were the files with copies of orders placed for this spring? Clarke always prepared orders during October for the following year, but Ellie couldn't find the records or copies of any paid invoices.

Had he intentionally left the business records in a mess so she would fail? And if he hadn't been calling on suppliers during October and November, where had he been all those afternoons?

That's a stupid question, she told herself. *One-word answer. Bambi!*

With one wide swing of her arm, Ellie knocked the work schedules off the table, sending a frightened Felix skidding down the hall and into the bedroom.

WHEN TRISH ARRIVED the next morning, she noticed the mess in Ellie's dining room, but didn't comment. She knew Ellie would tell her what was going on when she was ready.

Instead, she quizzed Ellie about the interview at the police department the day before. Ellie answered her questions but downplayed the entire situation—except for commenting on the perfect stroke of black eyeliner worn by the Legal Aid woman—one Bunny Maguire.

"Wait! They assigned Bunny to represent you!" Trish shrieked. "When did you plan to tell me that?"

Trish was dying to ask more, but she refrained from speaking—for thirty seconds. "Clarke's former attorney is representing you in a police investigation into Clarke's disappearance?" she asked.

"Looks like," Ellie said. "Can we talk about this later? If I don't concentrate on running the nursery right now, I won't have a paycheck to use to pay my miniscule percent of Hot Shot Maguire's fee."

"Right," Trish said. "We'll talk plants. But, it won't be half as interesting," Trish said quietly.

"You know anybody looking for a job?" Ellie asked.

"Does the question have anything to do with the mess in your dining room? I could ask Carolyn Smith who her cleaning lady is."

"Forget the cleaning woman. And, who's Carolyn Smith?"

"New lady in the yellow house up the block. The place with the plastic lawn chairs and out-of-proportion blue shutters," Trish said. "Want me to call her?"

"*No* to Carolyn Smith and, *no* to a cleaning woman," Ellie said. "I started out today by trying to develop a reasonable work schedule for this spring at Gardens and Greens. But now I'm more worried that I can't find any

46

evidence that Clarke placed the spring orders for the nursery. We do that during late fall every year."

"I've always wondered. Did you name the nursery or did Clarke?"

"We kind of compromised. He wanted 'Plants and Supplies.' But, I ordered the business cards, knowing that he'd be too cheap to replace them with his choice of business name. Then I had the signs painted before he could come up with a third name choice."

"You used to have spunk."

"The longer Clarke and I were married, the easier it was to not make waves. We wouldn't be in this mess now if I'd paid more attention."

"Let's not panic," Trish said. "Maybe he switched the records to his computer and when we get to the nursery we'll find everything neatly stored in computer files instead of those manila ones on your floor."

"I suppose he could have made some of the orders by phone," Ellie said. "But we'd still need a note on a calendar so we'd know when to expect the deliveries. I don't even see a calendar book for this year."

"That could also be on his laptop," Trish said. But there was less conviction in her voice this time. "I say we drive down to the garden shop and see what your guy Santos knows. You said he's been receiving deliveries for you."

Ellie didn't answer.

"Get your coat," Trish said.

"I'm afraid of what we're going to discover. No inventory, no garden shop."

"We'll figure it out," Trish said.

"Remember, I'm giving up the house I love for the business."

"I'll drive."

WHEN TRISH STEERED the car into the narrow front entrance road leading to the nursery, she hit the brakes. The business sign was in place, but there was a chain stretched across the dirt road, preventing vehicles from driving into the nursery yard.

Ellie pulled her phone out of the pouch on the front of her sweatshirt and tapped in the phone number for the nursery.

She didn't know whether to be mad or glad when Santos picked up the phone and she heard "Gardens and Greens. How may I help you?"

He told Ellie to stay with the car and he'd come down to meet her. Ellie repeated the message to Trish, but they still didn't know what was going on at the business. They got out of the car and waited behind the chain that barricaded the entrance. Santos pulled up in the older company truck and motioned to the women to climb in. The paint on the vehicle was peeling, and Ellie knew from experience that they wouldn't be able to hear themselves talk above the engine noise. Santos pulled forward and Ellie saw why he had closed the nursery entrance for the day. A pile of bark mulch (top grade, cedar, she noticed) dwarfed the greenhouse that held the violets and pansies in spring. The pyramid of mulch also blocked the main entrance road for customers.

Ellie waited to talk until Santos shut off the noisy truck engine in front of the sales' office.

If Clarke hadn't been here to place orders, and she hadn't placed an order for mulc... she thought before she spoke.

"I give up. Why are we blocking our main entry with bark mulch?"

"My question too," Santos said.

"We only 'special order' *cedar* mulch," Ellie said. "This definitely looks and smells like cedar. And this much? What did the delivery truck driver say?"

"You know drivers. They bring what they're told to deliver. This one was leaving—after already dumping the mulch—when I arrived this morning. I motioned for him to stop and asked him about it. He yelled '*mucho* mulch,' and hit the gas pedal."

Santos hesitated and surveyed the tower of bark mulch.

"I don't know why the mulch people wouldn't have questioned an order this big. It's more than a year's worth of mulch for a business this size." He looked at the pyramid of bark again. "Plus, most of your customers are happy to buy low-grade fir mulch at Lowe's or Home Depot," he added.

"And this was delivered before business hours?" Ellie asked.

"It wasn't here when I left at six last night."

49

Ellie was fuming.

"First things first," she said, gaining control. "Call the backhoe operator. The number will be in the box file on Clarke's old office desk. I'll make a sign to direct customers to the side and back entrances for today only."

"Got it."

"Thanks, Santos. While I think of it, has anyone answered the 'help wanted' ad that Clarke said he'd put in the newspaper?" Ellie asked.

Trish was unusually quiet. She was watching Ellie in action as the new sole owner of the nursery operation.

"I'm not sure Clarke got around to calling the newspaper or contacting Craig's List," Santos said. "I reminded him again before he left."

Santos walked toward the office to try to find the phone number and line up a backhoe operator for the day.

"What can I do to help?" Trish asked.

"You and I are going to search this office and see if we can find records for the orders Clarke should have placed for this spring. Unless, that is, you'd like to help me kill him."

WHEN ELLIE RETURNED to the sales office, she re-thought her earlier decision about the bark mulch problem.

"Santos," she said. "Let's try to save some man hours where the bark mulch is concerned. When you reach the backhoe guy, please ask him to shift the mulch that's blocking the drive onto the north end of the paving.

There's no reason we can't have customers pull up on the paved area when they pick up the mulch they've ordered. We can move some of the garden statues to another location so there's room for buyers in pickup trucks to back up. Those that are waiting can park on that paved strip by the tool shed."

"Problem solved?" Trish asked.

"The first one is," Ellie said.

Ellie thought she'd made a good call on solving the mulch problem. The new plan would help the flow of traffic on the site. It gave those purchasing mulch a shady place to park while they waited for service.

There were probably other parts of the operation that could also be improved, she thought. But not today.

She picked up a pen in the office and jotted down the wording for the "help wanted" ads. She also asked Trish to remind her to place the ads before they shut down Clarke's computer at the end of the day.

With Trish there to help, Ellie hoped they'd find out what Clarke had ordered for last spring. Plus, they should find the paid invoices to go with those orders, she reminded herself. She felt calmer. She'd work some extra hours, hire two part-timers to help with the watering and maintenance, and the nursery would be ready for the flood of early spring gardeners who would start arriving in a month or so.

Clarke would have been crazy, she thought, to order a mountain of mulch and not order any of the river rock that their customers bought by the truck load to build walkways in Oregon's wet climate.

51

She looked around. Clarke's office was relatively tidy—if she ignored the used coffee mugs he had let collect on top of the tall file cabinet. There was a wooden desk with a second shorter file cabinet pushed up against the side of it. The room was large enough for a desk chair, two straight-back wood chairs, and a long, upholstered bench by the entry.

Trish was surveying the room also.

"Not even a clock or a poster on the walls. Doesn't that seem strange to you?" Trish asked.

"He used to have a photo of Toni on his desk. I guess it speaks well for him that he took that with him."

Trish pulled open the top desk drawer. Pencils, pens, a small hand-held calculator, and a framed photo of Antonia sat against the bottom of the scarred wooden drawer.

"The bastard," Ellie said.

"That's a little harsh. He didn't throw the picture away."

"You're on Clarke's side?" Ellie asked.

"No way. I was just trying to keep you from going ballistic before we even start this job. So, boss, where do we start?"

"Let's pull any paper file that has last fall's date on it. We have—or used to have—a system of labeling every file with the date, year and subject. So, if Clarke really did order that mulch mountain out front, there should be a file labeled with a date from this fall and the subject 'ground coverings.'"

"Sounds easy enough," Trish said as she scanned the first several files. "For what it's worth, though, so far this drawer doesn't have a single file dated after spring of last year."

"Try the drawer below."

"Those are from two or three years ago," Trish said.

"Same over here," Ellie reported as she slammed the top drawer in the taller file cabinet. "Did he take the current sales and ordering records with him? Who does that?"

"An ex-husband who's planning to open his own business in Colorado?" Trish suggested.

They heard a phone ring out by the cash register in the customer service area.

"Gardens and Greens. How may I help you?" Santos asked. Then the receiver clunked against the counter and he called in to Ellie. "It's your sweet Antonia," he said.

Trish had found the phone set in Clarke's office by then and handed the receiver to Ellie.

"Thanks, Santos. I've got it."

She waited to speak until she heard the click of the other old-fashioned desk phone being put back in place.

"Toni, I'm here. Is everything all right?"

"Why do you always start a conversation like that?" her daughter asked. "Of course, everything's OK." She hesitated. "Well, kind of OK."

"What's going on?" Trish asked.

"What's going on?" Ellie repeated into the phone.

"It's Dad," Toni said. "He's supposed to get here tonight as we agreed, but I haven't heard from him." Toni hesitated for a minute. "Oops! I guess I forgot to tell the police about our plans. They only asked me about the past two weeks or so."

"I'm sure your answers were fine," Ellie said. "Is your dad driving or flying in this evening?"

"Flying, Mom. Who would drive from Colorado this time of year? He sent me his flight schedule almost a month ago. He's supposed to land at PDX at five, and he said he'd take a taxi to the Swank and Swine to meet me for dinner at seven."

"Swank and Swine?" Ellie asked. "Why that place?"

"He chose it because it's near the airport."

"That sounds like fun," Ellie forced herself to say. She resisted saying that Clarke would be dining at the right trough. Swine!

"I texted him three times this week. Even if he doesn't check his phone, wouldn't you think he'd have called last night to say everything was still on? I don't want to be left sitting at a table at the restaurant and have him be a 'no show.'"

"I think he's probably just preoccupied. Do you still have the 'emergency credit card' that I gave you?" Ellie asked.

"Yeah, but I'm not going to eat dinner alone in a pricey place like that."

"Of course not. You said you like your roommate, Sarah. Why don't the two of you go to dinner at 7 p.m. like your dad told you. If he doesn't show, that credit card and I will pay for your dinners. I've been thinking that I should do something nice for you girls. And, Antonia, I'm sure your dad is fine. If you hear from him, let me know. And I'll call you if I hear anything."

"Mom, that restaurant isn't the kind of place Sarah and I or anyone else our age would eat."

"Do it for me?" Ellie asked.

"Why? You're not married to him anymore."

Ellie elected to ignore the comment. "Because I worry about your diet," she said. "And also because I'm certain your dad is just preoccupied and forgot to check back with you. He'll be eager to see you again."

She disconnected from the call.

"Something rocky in Colorado?" Trish asked.

"Toni was supposed to meet Clarke in Portland tonight and she hasn't heard from him for weeks. She wanted to know if she was supposed to assume he would still be flying into PDX today."

"It sounded like you gave her good advice," said Trish, who didn't bother to pretend that she hadn't heard every word of the conversation. "I know you, and you're not going to be able to concentrate until Toni calls you back tonight. Why don't we take Clarke's computer home with us and look for those order and invoice files at your house?"

"Have I ever told you that you're a perfect friend?" Ellie asked.

"Probably, but not often enough. Thanks anyway," Trish said. "I do remember that Clarke tended to run late. Remember when he was two hours late to his 40th Surprise Birthday Party? And by the time he arrived, all of us but you were too drunk to remember or care that it was his birthday."

"How could I forget that?"

"In fact, if you'd rather refer to him as your 'late husband,' I'd do it. You're an emancipated woman now—thanks to the *late* S.O.B."

"You're a perfect friend," Ellie repeated.

ELLIE TRIED to avoid thinking about Clarke being labeled a "missing person."

NOT my problem anymore, she thought.

Bambi reported his disappearance to the police in *both* Colorado and Oregon. If the woman had lost track of her husband, it certainly wasn't Ellie's concern. Let the police deal with Bambi.

It was strange, though, she thought. *If he'd planned to leave town, wouldn't he have mentioned it to the new wife? And, if something had happened to him, wouldn't someone in Colorado have known about that?*

TRISH LOCATED the files on Clarke's laptop computer. It helped that he had used the same year and subject codes that he and Ellie had used for the old paper

56

filing system. Both women were blurry-eyed from staring at the computer screen all afternoon and decided they'd open the stored computer files the next morning.

"Before I head home," Trish said, "I'm supposed to remind you to place those help-wanted ads."

"I've got a mind like a sieve," Ellie said. "When will I feel normal again?"

"It's called the 'Divorce Nutsies.' My sis said it took her six months to a year before she could operate without a written list."

Trish slipped out the front door, and Ellie took off her shoes and stretched out on the living room couch. Felix joined her, but he jumped back to the floor again when the home phone rang.

Ellie looked at her watch. She must have fallen asleep. It was ten p.m. She checked her phone and saw Antonia's number on the screen.

"Hi Honey. Did everything work out OK?"

"Yeah," her daughter said. "Sarah and I had an amazing dinner. I hope you don't mind that we ordered the flaming dessert. And, some cute older guys came to our table and talked to us."

"Was your Dad there on time?"

Ellie heard a muffled sob.

"He didn't come. I don't think he ever planned to come."

"We don't know that," Ellie said. "Maybe there was a longer lay-over between planes."

"More likely he's in Colorado, laying..."

"Don't be crass, Antonia."

The call disconnected.

Ellie couldn't stop thinking about the situation. Something seemed off. She accepted (most days) that Clarke could leave her and never look back. But Antonia? Why would he let down his daughter?

7

Ellie relaxed after finding the few online orders that Clarke had made for Gardens and Greens. He'd even labeled the file with a name that she and Trish could spot easily. There didn't seem to be any rhyme or reason, though, as to which orders he had elected to place for the approaching growing season.

"Let me just throw something out there," Trish said. "Is it possible that he re-ordered from the companies who contacted *him* by email, but he didn't initiate any calls to renew the other orders?"

"Give me a minute," Ellie said. She checked the orders that he had made and found every one of them was sent in response to an email from the supplier.

"You're good," she told Trish.

"If that's true, then," Trish said, "we start by printing copies of the email orders he made this fall. They'll all be dated."

"And, then what?"

"We pull the invoice files from the year before and match this fall's email orders against those. Then we—actually, *you*—wind up with a stack of last year's paid invoices with no matching order for this year. That'll give you a list of products to order for this year. You'll have the amount ordered, the cost and the company contact info on those invoices."

"Genius!" Ellie said. "And I can probably get everything delivered on the same timetable as last year. Remind me to pay you time and a half for today's work."

"Time and a half of zero is still zero," Trish said dryly.

"It's the thought that counts."

ELLIE SLEPT SOUNDLY for the first night in weeks. One of her major problems at the nursery was solved—guaranteeing adequate inventory for spring. Or, it would be by the end of tomorrow. Now she could concentrate on hiring part-time staff for spring and summer.

The advertising instructions online at Craig's List advised businesses to request applicants to send letters of interest and names of references to the email address of the business, rather than to a personal e-mail address. Ellie listed that same online address in the notice she paid for in the newspaper. One step at a time, she was entering the so-called Technology Age. And surprise, surprise. It wasn't as complicated as Clarke had led her to believe.

So, why, she wondered, *had Clarke insisted that he was the only person who was allowed to touch the company computer? Duh! The answer was obvious,* she thought. *Bambi.*

When she checked, she found that Clarke had deleted his personal email account. *Natch.*

Ellie heard a familiar ring tone and reached for her phone.

"What are you doing on Friday night?" Trish asked.

"Basking in the glory of having made some brilliant additions to the staff at the nursery." She hesitated. "I hope."

"You don't have plans after five?"

"No. What's up?"

"I've decided to throw you a divorce party," Trish said.

"That would be a 'no!' A loud NO!"

"It would do you good. We can get together with some friends and exchange divorce horror stories. It'll be a hoot," she added. "And all you have to do is show up at my place at eight o'clock."

"I know your heart's in the right place," Ellie said. "But, I'm begging you. Please don't. Those women are already a few years removed from the betrayal. I'm still pretty ragged."

"Damn. When I mentioned the party plan to my mom, she said you might be a little raw yet. Why is my mother still always right?"

"I don't know," Ellie said. "But if you get a chance, you might drop that line about mothers always being right into a conversation with Toni."

"How's Toni doing?"

"Hurting, but not talking."

THE FIRST POSSIBLE new hire for the nursery was a woman attending Oregon State University and majoring in horticulture. This applicant was willing to work late afternoons until closing time on weekdays, which would free Ellie during some of those hours to oversee orders and payroll. The woman answered all the interview questions satisfactorily. Plus, she seemed to be naturally cheerful and not afraid to get her hands dirty. If the calls to references were promising, Ellie planned to hire her.

"Yesterday's other two candidates washed out," Ellie later told Trish.

"How can you wash out as a plant waterer?"

"One of them couldn't lift anything over ten pounds. Do you know what a recently watered potted plant weighs?"

"And, the other one?" Trish asked.

"I know I'm out of practice, but I think he was hitting on me."

"Go, Ellie!" Trish said.

Ellie ignored the outburst. "Then, today's first job candidate was a *no show*," Ellie continued. "Who does that?" she asked. "But wait till I tell you about the second one."

"I'm waiting."

"The man showed up twenty minutes early for his interview and asked if he could tour the outdoor stock areas. He said he wanted to get an idea of the general setup of what he hoped would be his future place of employment," Ellie reported to Trish.

"And?"

"His interview went well," Ellie said, "but I sensed he was either nervous or not used to applying for work."

"Either is possible."

"So I asked him if he had any questions for me," Ellie said.

"I repeat myself. 'And?'"

"He asked if we require a criminal background check before hiring someone."

"That's interesting," Trish said.

"It gets way beyond 'interesting,'" Ellie said. "Next, he told me that he had been arrested early last year."

"We pick 'em," Trish said.

"Of course, I'm sitting there thinking I might be interviewing an axe murderer. Then he said, 'I don't believe the circumstances would affect your hiring decision, but I want to be candid.'"

"Were you ready to run?" Trish asked.

63

"I was trying to keep my cool while I estimated the number of steps to the door."

"How was that going?" Trish asked.

"He said he was cited and released for harassment and possible fraud. 'The fraud charge was later dropped,' he told me."

"Tell me there were extenuating circumstances," Trish said.

"You sound like an attorney," Ellie answered. "He said he was in the middle of a divorce and he let anger cloud his judgment. When he got into his wife's car one morning, he saw her boyfriend's credit card on the floor between the front seats."

Trish leaned forward, waiting to hear more.

"He went on Amazon.com and ordered over $1,500 worth of merchandise in thirty-some separate orders—*all* to be delivered to the new Mr. Wonderful's home address and *all* charged to the guy's credit card. He said he had no idea purchases of lingerie would add up that fast."

"I told you divorce stories are good," Trish said. "How did you keep a straight face?"

"I'm afraid I didn't. I wanted to yell 'you're hired!'" Ellie said. "Instead, I thanked him for coming and told him I'd need to check references and then get back to him."

"What's his name?" Trish asked.

"Rod Nelson."

"Hire him!" Trish said.

"Because you like his name?"

"No. Because he's upfront about his past," Trish said.

"I probably will. He's no kid. He's around our age."

"Perfect."

"Both the people he listed as references raved about his work ethic and generally thought he was great," Ellie said.

"He could have faked his references. It has been known to happen."

"No. I knew two of the people he listed."

"And?"

"The first one was the supervisor at his weekday job. Rod teaches middle school PE."

"That leaves him weekends to work another job," Trish said.

"Exactly."

"Is there anything stopping you?"

"The school principal mentioned 'off the record' that she had heard that Mr. Nelson had racked up a lot of legal fees during a recent divorce."

"Was it ethical for her to tell you that?" Trish asked.

"Probably not, but I think she was pulling for me to offer him the job."

"And the other reference?" Trish asked.

"Mayor William Thompson gave him a glowing endorsement."

"Now I'm confused. Did you hire the college-aged woman also?" Trish asked.

"Yes. I suspect they'd work well together if they ever wind up on the same shift. For now, the new woman is working weekdays and Mr. Nelson is working on the weekends."

"Does she have a name?"

"Kristi. Kristi Smith."

8

Ellie had her coat on, ready to go out the door to work, when the home phone rang. She stopped by the small table in the front entryway to take the call. She recognized the number displayed on caller ID.

"What are you doing up this early?" she asked Toni.

"Thack is taking me to breakfast," her daughter said.

"Thack?"

"Well, Thackery," Toni said. "I met him Wednesday night at a dinner at the dorm. You'd like him. He's a freshman, but he's older. And the neat part, Mom, is that he's a foreign student here on a student visa. He's from Myanmar."

"Where did you say this Hickory is from?" Ellie asked as she balanced the phone on her shoulder.

67

"Thackery! Not 'Hickory,' Mom. You're such a bigot!"

"I wasn't being a bigot, honey." *And what would be racist about the name Hickory anyway*, Ellie wondered. "I work at a nursery. It was a natural mistake."

"Yeah, right."

"And I have to confess that I don't remember where Myanmar is on a world map."

"'Burma' to your generation," Toni said. "This call was a mistake."

"Toni, I work with trees and plants. I apologize if what I said sounded racist to you. And I'm glad you met someone nice."

"He's more than *nice*, Mom. 'Nice' is probably what you called Dad when you met him."

"Sexy?"

Toni laughed. "There's no hope for you, Mom. I called to tell you that I'm feeling the happiest I've felt since Dad stood me up."

"That's great. I'm not sure I'm comfortable with you dating someone older."

"Yeah. Whatever," Toni said. The call ended.

Ellie was on the front porch of her home with the exterior door locked, leaving for work, when she heard the land line ring again.

Doesn't everyone but telemarketers use cell phones now? Ellie thought. *If it's Toni calling back, she knows my mobile number.*

SANTOS PEREZ ARRIVED first at the nursery each morning and did some janitorial chores before the sales operation opened at eight. Ellie didn't have to rush, she reminded herself, and glanced at the speedometer.

She looked in the rearview mirror and saw flashing lights approaching her Honda Civic. (Clarke got the more valuable vehicle, but she kept the more reliable one.) She gritted her teeth now and pulled over as far to the right as she could and brought the car to a stop.

An unmarked police car, followed by an ambulance and a "lit up" Benton County sheriff's car, flew past her as morning commuters going in both directions parted for the emergency vehicles.

It took a minute or two for Ellie's heartbeat to return to normal after her initial reaction that the police had been headed her way to ticket her for speeding. She took two deep breaths and then pulled her car out slowly and safely onto the road.

Ellie glanced over her shoulder two minutes later and saw a fire truck, its lights getting brighter and the siren growing louder as it gained speed. She thought she also heard her cell phone ring, but the tone was hard to distinguish when blended with the sound of sirens. She pulled to the side of the road again.

This is convenient, she told herself as she reached for the phone. Oregon law required that she pull off the road anyway and come to a complete stop to answer a hand-held cell phone. She reminded herself to stop by the Honda sales office in town and have someone there show her how to hook up Bluetooth so she could answer the call "hands free." *One of the many tasks her once-caring husband should have taken care of before he left,* she thought.

"It's Santos."

"Yes, Santos. What is it?" Ellie asked.

"The police are here. I called them. You need to come to the back entrance. Nobody comes in from the front or side driveways, they say."

"I'm almost there. Is everyone OK? I don't see any flames."

Ellie heard someone in the background speaking to Santos.

"Gotta go," Santos said. "But I'll see you in a few minutes."

Two more drivers had passed Ellie's car and then pulled their vehicles to the right and onto the dirt siding in front of where she was parked. She noticed that the car directly in front of her had California plates. Oregonians grumbled about the increasing population in their state as Californians moved north. *None, though,* she thought, *ever hesitated to accept full-price offers from the newcomers looking for housing. Maybe, if she did have to sell her house, she could find a realtor who catered to out-of-state buyers.* Finances were never far from her mind since the divorce.

Several decades ago, tasteless bumper stickers proclaiming *"Don't Californicate Oregon"* had shown up on a smattering of Oregon vehicles. Ellie hadn't seen one of the stickers for a few years. Either the sentiment had changed, or Oregon rain had slowly dissolved the bumper statements.

She heard engines starting and saw the two cars that had been idling ahead of her swoop back into traffic. She took one more look in her driver's side mirror before joining them on the highway. She replayed the phone call from the nursery in her mind.

THE HEADLIGHTS of Ellie's car swept the back driveway as she turned into the nursery, and she could see a police officer, motioning her to slow down. When she stopped the car and stepped out, the officer signaled her to halt. He verified her name and then helped her across the muddy ground and toward the sales office.

The new woman employee isn't due to report for work until Monday, Ellie thought, *and New Guy Rod won't arrive until next Saturday. What could have caused all this commotion?*

Drivers of the emergency vehicles that passed her on the road had all parked at the front entrance. Red and blue emergency lights flashed across the outdoor sales yard.

"Mrs. Mobley?" the policeman said. "I'm Detective Buchanan."

"It's *Ms.* Mobley, for now," she corrected him. She had an appointment scheduled with Bunny Maguire next week to file the paperwork to reclaim her maiden name.

"That's not important right now," he said brusquely. "We have a situation here. And we're not sure if it's a matter of life and death or a sick prank."

71

"What's happened?"

"It's difficult to see from here, but there's a possible crime scene at the front entrance to your business."

"See what? What's going on?" Ellie asked.

Santos was bent over in the doorway, scraping some of the mud from his shoes with an old trowel. Neither man answered her question instantly.

"I have a few questions first," the detective said. "Your employee Santos Perez told me you weren't expecting two orders of bark mulch to be delivered after dark this week. Can you verify that?'

"Of course. Santos is correct. He oversees all our deliveries. Has bark mulch been made illegal in this state or something? Are the environmentalists at it again?"

"No Ma'am. No on both counts."

"Wait a minute. There's been a *second* delivery?"

"That's affirmative," the man answered, never losing his official tone of voice.

"Detective," she said. "I'm already late for work and, for what it's worth, I'm not finding any of this amusing."

"We certainly aren't either," he said. "Far from it."

Ellie looked confused. She stared at the detective. "There's something you haven't had time to tell me, isn't there? What don't I know?" she asked meekly.

"Your employee, Santos Perez, called the police department immediately upon arriving this morning. The call came in at 6:53 a.m.," he said, glancing down at a pocket-sized tablet of notes he had apparently taken after receiving the early morning call. "This is an unusual situation."

"Unusual?" she prompted again.

"Mr. Perez spotted something sticking out from under the latest bark delivery. The pile nearest the road," he said.

"And?"

"We have crime scene investigators down there now excavating as quickly and safely as they can. They had to build wood braces first to secure the mound of mulch." He looked at Ellie again. "Maybe you should sit down," he suggested.

"I'm OK here at the sales counter," she said.

"Suit yourself. Is there anyone who would want to do you or your husband harm?"

Whoa. That was a big jump, she thought.

"Not that I know of," she said. "My *ex*-husband lives in Colorado."

"Was yours a civil divorce?" he asked.

"Absolutely not."

The detective was startled by the response but remained quiet.

"It was a *civil* court proceeding, if that's what you meant," Ellie said. "But the marriage didn't end with either one of us suggesting we all get together for summer vacations to sing *Oh Susannah* around the campfire."

The man relaxed his pose slightly. "Is there any 'beef' with any of the trucking firms that deliver merchandise here?" he asked.

"Absolutely not."

Detective Buchanan noted her use of the phrase again. It could be a speech pattern for this woman rather than a reflection of anger, he thought.

"Clarke," she said. "He was my husband..."

"Got it."

"Clarke did the ordering, but we contract with an outfit like PayPal that issues payment to each supplier and sends us stamped 'paid' invoices online along with the total we owe. There shouldn't be any ill will with the suppliers or drivers. There hasn't been in the past."

Ellie mentally listed the sketchy details she'd heard so far from the detective and tried to stay calm. *Why all the emergency vehicles?* she wondered.

"What haven't you told me?" she asked.

"Mr. Perez spotted something unusual sticking out of the bottom of your latest bark mulch delivery. That's why he called us," the detective repeated.

Could the detective please get to the point? she wondered.

"Mr. Perez believes the men's boots sticking out from under the mulch belong to your ex-husband. He said Clarke Mobley wears distinctive boots."

"He does." Ellie hesitated. "Did?"

"Let's say 'does' for now," the detective answered. "Once again. Had you ordered any bark?"

"That's a little hard for me to answer. Clarke, my *ex*-husband, had placed the orders until recently."

Ellie noticed that the sun was coming up. On any other morning, she'd be opening the nursery for business now.

"Which day did the first load of mulch arrive? We need specifics during a crime scene interview," Buchanan said.

"You're *interviewing* me?"

"I introduced myself earlier," he said. "Before asking you any questions."

"If this is Clarke's attempt to put me out of business, I'm going to kill him," Ellie said.

The detective took a step back in the small space. He straightened his shoulders. "I'm going to ask that you don't say anything else right now," he said. "Remain silent. I want to warn you against incriminating yourself either accidentally or willfully."

Ellie couldn't believe what she was hearing. The detective was reciting the Miranda rights. Santos reached for a hardback office chair and slid it across the floor and against the back of Ellie's knees. She sat.

"Do you understand those rights?" the detective asked.

"Yes," she said quietly.

"It's very possible there's more than boots buried under the latest mulch pile."

Ellie paled.

"I've shoveled a lot of mulch," she said. "When it's wet, it's incredibly heavy. How could anyone survive being buried under that?"

"We don't know," Buchanan said. "We do know there are amazing tales of people being pulled out alive from beneath rubble following earthquakes. Or surviving being buried in snow because there was an air pocket. Our job right now is to stay out of the way of the emergency crews. And to think positive thoughts."

Ellie looked down at the floor. A small sob escaped her mouth.

"I understand that you're upset," the detective said. "Sometimes these calls end positively. I'll walk down there in a couple of minutes and see what I can learn."

"Had the delivery truck already left by the time you got here?" Ellie asked Santos.

He nodded "yes.'

"Is there anyone we could call for you, Mrs. Mobley?" the detective asked. Ellie noticed the man had become less hostile. Maybe he was just doing his job earlier. *What a terrible job to have,* she thought.

"My daughter, Antonia, is at PSU." Ellie hesitated. "But, I don't want to call her until we know something definite. I talked to her by phone this morning."

"What time was the call?" the detective asked.

"Six fiftyish. I was walking out the door and turned around to catch the call. We didn't talk long. I heard the desk phone ring again after I'd locked the door to leave, but I didn't go back."

"That could have been *my* first call," Santos said. "I didn't leave a message."

"Surely there's a friend or relative you'd like one of us to call for you," the detective said.

"Maybe your friend Trish who helped you with the invoices?" Santos asked.

The detective started toward the door, then came to a sudden stop. He remembered talking to other officers during the initial missing person report on Clarke Mobley. Buchanan cleared his throat.

"You might want to give that firecracker attorney of yours a call," he said to Ellie.

Obviously, word had spread through the police department about her representation by Bunny Maguire.

THE ENGINE NOISE near the front driveway shut off, leaving an eerie quiet on the site. Buchanan stepped into the nursery yard to speak with a crew member who was walking toward the sales office.

Ellie thought the conversation was taking too long if all the man had to say was "sick joke." She heard an engine turn over and the crew from the fire truck climbed aboard to leave the scene.

Buchanan walked back to the sales area where Ellie and Santos waited.

"We may have an answer," Buchanan said quietly. "I'll be back to let you know as soon as we have details confirmed."

"That's all you can say?" Ellie asked.

"There's a man..."

Ellie wasn't sure if she was screaming or if someone else was making that high-pitched noise. Santos dropped a cup of coffee and it shattered on the cement floor. None of them moved to clean up the liquid and shards of pottery.

"Is it Clarke?" Ellie asked quietly.

"We haven't confirmed that, ma'am. Some of this is difficult," the detective said from the doorway.

"Just tell me," she said.

"The victim appears to be unclothed," Buchanan said. "Except for the boots."

The room was quiet.

"Mrs. Mobley, do you carry a photo of your ex-husband in your wallet?"

Ellie stared at him.

"Right," he said. "Absolutely not?"

Ellie nodded. *Does anybody carry a photo of an ex-husband?*

"Mr. Perez, would you recognize Mr. Mobley? By now they've probably cleared off the mulch near the body."

Santos nodded and moved to the door, and the two men left the office area and headed toward the site where the digging crew had gathered.

The workmen were roping off the lower part of the nursery yard with yellow crime scene tape. Emergency vehicles had backed over some young trees in the crews' haste to arrive. Mulch was everywhere. Two diggers were now tackling the first mulch pile with shovels to make sure there was nothing but bark in that delivery.

Detective Buchanan moved in closer to view the body. He motioned to Santos to join him.

SANTOS RETURNED and solemnly entered the sales office where Ellie waited. He thought the detective would be there already. *Wasn't it the policeman's job to share this information with the victim's wife?*

He glanced around. Still no detective. *Oh, hell,* he thought.

"I'm so sorry," he said. And then, softly in Spanish, *"Lo siento."*

Ellie waited for him to continue.

"It's Clarke," he said quietly.

Santos had stopped to retrieve a thermos of coffee from his work truck, and now he poured a cup for Ellie and another for himself. He had hoped that the few minutes it took to stop by his truck would have given the detective enough time to return to the sales office and tell Mrs. Mobley that Clarke was dead.

"They think the heavy rain splashing on the ground uncovered the boots," he added.

Damn, he thought again. *This sort of thing isn't part of my job. Where's the detective?*

"Clarke's supposed to be in Colorado with what's-her-name," Ellie said.

There was no noise coming from the excavation site now. Only an eerie quiet.

"Your Trish is coming. I reached her on my phone," Santos said. "You gave me her name and number in case of emergencies after Clarke left."

"Thank you. What did you tell her?" Ellie asked.

"Only that you need her here. Now."

"Thank you, Santos." Ellie sipped the hot coffee carefully. "Are you OK?" she asked.

Santos nodded. "I think so," he said.

"You did everything right this morning," she told him. "I don't know what I would have done if I'd been the first one here."

The two of them sat together quietly for five minutes before Santos saw Buchanan returning. He cursed the detective silently and moved aside for the man to enter the room. Santos glared at the detective and reported that he had reached a friend to be with Mrs. Mobley.

Santos wasn't sure what his place was now. He moved toward the door and the detective made no attempt to stop him from leaving. He busied himself cleaning up the yard near the sales office so things would look tidy when it would eventually be time to reopen the nursery. Obviously, the business would be closed today. Possibly all week.

He saw Trish trotting toward the sales office where the detective and Ellie were waiting for word that the coroner was there to transport Clarke Mobley to the morgue.

Trish entered the room and Ellie introduced her. She glanced from Ellie to the detective. "What gives?" she asked.

"The facts are..." The dectective stopped short. "I want you to listen carefully and try not to respond in a manner that will be upsetting to your friend," he said, remembering Ellie's earlier scream.

"Of course."

"There is a deceased male buried under a pile of bark mulch that was delivered early this morning," he said.

"What?" Trish asked. "I mean *who*?"

"The deceased has been *tentatively* identified as Clarke Eldridge Mobley. And I stress that's a tentative ID."

"Wishes do come true," Trish said under her breath.

"I beg your pardon?" the detective asked.

"Nothing. It was nothing," Trish answered quietly. She was ashamed of her first reaction.

The detective pulled a small notebook from his uniform pocket. "Could you spell your full name for me please?" he asked Trish.

"Why do you need that? I'm Ellie's friend."

"You, Ms. Grover, are also the third possible suspect I've interviewed this morning. There's Mrs. Mobley, her employee Mr. Perez, and now *you*."

"Hey!" Trish yelled.

"Plus, someone mentioned a daughter. Antonia?"

"No way," the women said in unison.

"I wouldn't be overly concerned about being early suspects," the detective told them. "Everyone on scene when we arrive at a felony is initially a suspect."

For once, Trish was speechless.

"My friend's name is Patricia Grover," Ellie said. "That's G-r-o-v-e-r."

"And," Trish added, "*her* attorney's name is Bunny Maguire. That's B-u-n-n-y. And, I'm calling Ms. Maguire. Now!"

"In the case of a possible murder, the suspect list could grow to twenty-five or more," the detective said.

"That's supposed to make us feel better?"

Detective Buchanan arranged for an officer to drive the women home.

"Have someone pick up your cars for you later," he told Ellie. "You probably shouldn't drive today."

"THE MINUTE I got home, I told Harvey about what had happened at the nursery," Trish said.

"Of course. Clarke was his friend, too."

"He brought up something I hadn't thought about. Would you like me to stay with you for a couple of nights?" Trish asked. "I'm not going anywhere until Harv makes arrangements to pick up the cars for us."

"Thanks. But I don't know that it's necessary for me to have a 'keeper.'"

"I'm not moving in forever," Trish said. "I thought maybe for a couple of nights is all. It creeps me out that whoever did that to Clarke might know where you live."

"Geez. That thought hadn't occurred to me."

"I'll be over tonight about eight," Trish said.

ELLIE WELCOMED HER overnight guest. As the day progressed, Ellie had realized how much she didn't want to be alone tonight. She made hot tea and Trish arrived with a supply of donut holes. They never got around to turning on the television. There was too much floating through their minds about everything that had happened since Clarke's untimely and strange exit.

"Is it just me, or is Bunny growing on us—in a good way?" Trish asked.

"What would be a bad way?" Ellie wanted to know.

"A skin disease? A tumor? Poison ivy? I don't know."

"Well, she does have a habit of showing up right behind the cops. I love the way she dresses. Professional, but with a little edge," Ellie said. "Plus, she never turns down baked goods. So, yes. I do think I could like her."

Trish popped another donut hole in her mouth. "She's tough, but not cheap like her sister, whose name I refuse to utter."

Ellie looked up with a sly smile. "You suppose Mumsy was a tramp and those two have different fathers?"

"No. Same last name. And they look enough alike to be twins. One's the Evil Twin and the other's The Good Witch," Trish said. "But I'm proud of you. That's the first really catty remark I've heard you make since all this started."

"I love the way Bunny walks into a room and the cops forget their intimidation act. 'Oh, no need to interview you today while you're upset. Can we get you anything? Would you like to go home and take a nap before we continue?'" Ellie mimicked.

"Do you have another appointment with the Men in Blue?"

"I'm going to the Police Station Wednesday at eleven," Ellie said. "Speaking of the Good Witch... Bunny is picking me up. She's still determined that I just sit there and say nothing. It's so hard when I want to shout out 'If I'd wanted him dead, I'd have killed him months ago when he first told me he was leaving."

"Probably best if you wait until Bunny is there to guide your responses."

"Have I told you what I saw on Dateline on TV?" Ellie asked. "There's apparently a way you can sit on someone's chest until they lose consciousness and then smother them with a pillow without leaving any marks."

"Do *not* mention your TV viewing habits aloud. *Ever!*"

"But, did I do that to Clarke?" Ellie continued. "I did not. I simply bawled for days on end and looked through our wedding album and at Toni's baby photos for hours, trying to figure out why I was so damned happy with such a schmuck."

"I'm glad I came over," Trish said. "I think you needed this little talk therapy session."

Ellie stretched and yawned. "And I'll tell you what I think. I think Mrs. Mobley Number Two might have seen the light much sooner than I did and killed him. Or she had one of her other boyfriends knock him off."

"No more Dateline for you," Trish said.

9

Santos continued to open the nursery each morning, but he seemed much more solemn to Ellie. She tried to treat him in the same manner as always, but she realized that neither of their lives would ever be quite the same.

Santos had confessed to Ellie that being interviewed by the police scared him. While *he* was a US citizen, he said, some of his family members were not. He was concerned that the police investigation might extend to interviewing his relatives.

Ellie knew that both she and Santos were still considered suspects—no matter how far-fetched that might be—and being interviewed by the police still weighed heavily on Santos.

ELLIE PULLED TWO dining room chairs and a small end table out on the patio Saturday. It was 11 a.m. and she and Trish had already consumed a day's calories in Pepsi and Wheat Thins with peanut butter.

"Don't sweat it," Trish said. "Wheat Thins didn't get their name by being high calorie."

"I don't think the bakers plan on people consuming half a box each on a weekend morning."

"What does Saturday have to do with it?" Trish asked.

"Nothing I can think of."

"Right! Pass me the peanut butter."

Neither woman was particularly concerned about the number reflected on the bathroom scale. Ellie had stopped trying to meet Clarke's standards after she saw the pencil-thin Bambi.

"It must have been a drought year in the forest when Bambi was born," she'd told Trish.

"The nice thing is when we go to the doctor at this age, no one quizzes us about possible anorexia or bulimia."

"Small comfort," Ellie said quietly.

"Have I ever told you about my first husband?" Trish asked.

"No. I forgot there was anybody before Harvey."

"I was twenty when we met. He was eight years older and we were married less than a year."

"What happened to this older mystery man?" Ellie asked.

"He's lucky I didn't murder him."

"Don't use the 'm' word," Ellie cautioned. "We never know when a detective might be lurking about the yard."

"Husband Numero Uno and I had been married for under a year when an invitation arrived for his high school class reunion. I thought it would be fun to go and meet some of his friends and he didn't seem opposed to the idea. The thought even crossed my mind that he might want to show off his young wife to his high school buddies."

"And?" Ellie asked.

"Let me give you the *Readers' Digest* condensed version. He was out on the dance floor at the reunion 'feeling up' his high school girlfriend. And that was before any alcohol was served."

"Now I know why you never shared the story. What did you do?"

"I did what any other sound-thinking 19-year-old would have done. I walked out to the middle of the dance floor and threw a plastic cup full of bright pink punch toward his crotch. There was a little left in the cup, so I splashed it down the plunging neckline of the woman's white dress. Then I drove the car home, leaving him stranded with High School Tootsie."

"Good for you. See? You've always had guts."

89

"The story's not over. I drove home, as I said, and moved all his belongings—furniture, sports equipment, clothing—out on the front lawn. I worked all damned night. As soon as the sun came up, I started calling locksmiths to see how soon I could get the locks on the house changed. For a little extra money, those guys are incredibly quick."

"Perfect! Did you ever see him again?"

"Only from behind as he gathered up his stuff and put it in the back of a high school buddy's pickup truck. It took them two loads. Unfortunately, the sprinkler system miraculously came on while they were on the lawn."

"Don't you hate it when that happens?"

"He was served with divorce papers ten days later—and the attorney my dad paid for arranged it so I didn't even have to see the jerk in court."

"Sweet," Ellie said.

"We didn't have kids. We lived in a rental house. I had a friend from work who offered to return the wedding gifts from El Jerko's side of the family."

"And you never looked back?" Ellie asked.

"Nope. I sent in my college application the next day. Five years later, I met Harvey while I was working on campus after my senior year at UC Santa Barbara."

"Well, you got a winner the second time."

"Which reminds me. Harv says to let him know if you need any help with the yard while the house is on the market."

Harvey's very appearance signaled "stability." He was about five feet nine and had a stocky build. And he smiled day and night. His shaved head popped out of Lands' End catalogue shirts. Chinos and loafer-style shoes added to the "dependable" image. Trish and Ellie both knew he was "Mr. Reliable," but Ellie would call him only as a last resort. She was concentrating on being independent. Not by choice, but to stay sane.

The women moved inside to top off the morning snack with an official lunch.

"Do you think the cops are idle or do they not feel obligated to keep me posted on the investigation into Clarke's death?" Ellie asked.

"The second," Trish answered.

"That's rude. In any other line of work, people keep you posted on their progress. If I take a chair to the upholstery shop and there's going to be a delay, the guy calls me. If I schedule a painter and he realizes his current job is going to flop over into the next day, he lets me know."

"This is a little bit—no, a lot—different. The man was covered in mulch, not chintz."

"True. But I woke up in the middle of the night thinking that you and I should be looking for the killer."

"Hold on a minute," Trish said. "Do I sense role reversal here? You're supposed to be the timid, polite one in this friendship. I'm the one who charges ahead without thinking. Aren't you the one whose standard answer is 'this may not be such a good idea'?"

91

"That would be me. But, I can't sit around here waiting to hear that the detective has decided that Antonia or I killed Clarke." Ellie took a breath. "And I'm not sure that you're not a prime suspect also."

"You don't truly think he suspects me, do you?"

"No. But I didn't think that Clarke would file for divorce either. And we both know how that turned out."

Trish was quiet for a minute. "OK," she said. "Why don't we do our own detective work? We'll need some supplies, though. Let's start with a pad of paper and a pencil and map out our first logical steps. Step One?"

"I don't have a clue," Ellie said. "But I'll work 24 hours a day to make sure Toni isn't treated like a suspect by the police. She's had a rough enough time with this. Don't newspaper and TV reporters realize that victims have families? Why can't they leave it at 'found dead'? No. They have to go into sordid detail about a human smothered in mulch, the temperature of the body…"

Trish put an arm around her friend.

"Sorry. I got a little carried away," Ellie said.

"No need to be sorry. You need to let it out," Trish said. "And talking to Felix at night doesn't count."

"Back to business," Ellie said.

"OK. Think of all the old TV detective series. If Columbo or Rockford were still alive, where would they start?"

"With clichés?" Ellie asked.

"Precisely. So, Number One on our plan can be to find out if it's true that the killer always returns to the scene of the crime."

"Pardon my naiveté, but how do we determine *that*?" Ellie asked.

"We stake out the nursery for the next few nights. We watch to see if there are any nocturnal visitors there in addition to the deer feeding on the spring shoots on the rose bushes."

"Do you think anyone would drive up the driveway if the 'we're closed' sign is hanging out front?"

"We can't answer that sitting here. If we stake out the place, at the very least we might find out who's delivering truckloads of mulch that you haven't ordered."

"True. But do we think someone will pull in if my car is there?"

"We'll take my car," Trish said. "That's about the only advantage to having a black car. I don't think it outweighs how often I need to wash it or that I burn my buns on the hot leather seats in summer. But, the color works in our favor this time. We can park beyond that small grove of trees."

"What do we do while we're there?"

"We watch. We listen. And we look for any odd patterns of behavior. For instance, pedestrians cutting through as a short cut to the mini-market up the road. Or drunks heading to that bar and pool hall about three miles up. How do I know? You may even have teenage couples bedding down among the nursery shrubs. Then, we wait until they're out by the highway, and we stop them and ask if they've seen anything unusual at the nursery after dark."

"You think all these things actually occur?" Ellie asked. "Nightly?"

"Ellie, we won't know that, will we, unless our little surveillance team checks it out?"

"Agreed."

They also agreed any good game plan needed at least three steps.

"It's like a recipe," Trish said. "You can't stop after 'preheat the oven to 375 degrees Fahrenheit' if you hope to accomplish anything."

"We need suspects," Ellie said. "In addition to anyone we may meet during the stakeout, that is. How many nights do we have to hide out at the nursery?"

"It's pretty cold this week. I'd think three or four nights would be adequate. We're looking for patterns here."

"Then we can add the names of anybody we see at the nursery to our suspect list," Ellie said. "I am right, aren't I? We're not going to 'apprehend' any of these people roaming around in the middle of the night, are we?"

"Let's not get ahead of ourselves."

THE GROUNDS at the nursery showed evidence of a combination of careful planning and rapid growth. Ellie and Clarke had mapped the areas in advance, adding each new set of parking spaces as they were able to afford to hire the backhoe operator to clear the area and the construction crew to lay the paving and construct a gate.

By the time of the Mobley divorce, there was the conventional front gate with limited parking just inside the nursery yard, plus an area on the west side for parking for customers. The small parking lot behind was filled primarily with cars driven by employees or drivers of local delivery vans.

Ellie now marveled at the height of the trees she and Clarke had planted the first two years the nursery was in operation. These trees weren't part of the sales stock, but rather those they had placed strategically to provide shade on parts of the outdoor nursery yard. In addition to the small grove that shielded Trish's car the nights of the stakeouts, there was another group behind a year-round display of outdoor birdbaths and statuary.

A third stand of evergreen trees had been planted to shield the muddy and unsightly nursery equipment from neighboring properties. Ellie liked to think that near-by neighbors preferred to give directions to their homes when they could say "we're just west of that pretty plant nursery." She suspected few would be as thrilled saying "watch for the muddy yellow backhoes and turn right at the next driveway."

She also hoped the line of forsythias along the fence kept the bags of fertilizer out of sight and smell range. She couldn't do anything about the native skunks that toured the grounds after dark. Not to mention annual raccoon conventions held during mid-summer nights...

THE PHONE woke Ellie.

"Buchanan here, Mrs. Mobley."

"*Ms.* Mobley," she said automatically. "And do you always start your day at..." She glanced at the clock and said "...*before* 7 a.m.?"

"Good morning, Ma'am. I need to talk to both you and Mrs. Grover before you leave the house today."

"Are you asking me to come to the police station?"

"No, I'm coming your way. I just talked to Mrs. Grover on the phone. Can you meet me at her residence in, say, twenty minutes?"

"Absolutely," Ellie said.

"That is, if you want to see me with no makeup and messy hair," she said to herself.

"And, we'll assume the good detective won't mind me wearing yesterday's dirty jeans and sweatshirt," she told Felix.

The cat cuddled back into the covers.

"Fine," Ellie said. "You make the bed when you get up, though." She took a minute to rub Felix under the chin before rummaging around the room to find something clean to wear.

The phone rang again. *"Trish,"* Ellie thought.

"He told me not to contact you before he arrived," Trish said.

"Me too. He couldn't possibly have thought *that* was going to happen."

"No," they said together.

"I've got coffee over here," Trish said. "Any chance you have creamer?"

"I'm on my way. Or am I supposed to wait until Detective Buchanan pulls up out front?'

"Should we call Bunny?"

"We'll play it by ear. Get your backside over here."

BUCHANAN WENT through the formalities when he arrived. Yes, the women understood that this was a formal police investigation. Yes, they remembered that they had been briefed on the circumstances surrounding the death of Clarke Mobley at the Gardens and Greens nursery.

"And," the detective finished, "you women do remember that anything you say can and will be held against you in a court of law?"

"Absolutely," they said together.

"Just curious. Are you two sisters?"

"Not," they said at the same time.

"Why would you think that?" Trish asked.

"Sometimes you respond in 'twin talk.' I've never heard that before between friends."

"Could we just get to the point?" Trish asked. "I have to take the car in to be serviced at 10:30 this morning."

"Then, my timing's good. There were lots of tire tracks in the back driveway at the nursery the night of Mr. Mobley's death. We've attributed most of those tracks to nursery trucks and emergency vehicles. But, there's one very distinct set we've yet to identify. Could you tell me what kind of cars you drive?"

"Honda Civic," Ellie said.

"Dusty Ford Escape," her friend answered.

"I doubt the tires on either one of those will match the evidence left at the scene, but I'd like to look anyway."

"Be our guest," Trish said.

As they walked outside to Trish's driveway, the detective flipped through his cell phone until he found a photo of the tire tracks in question. He didn't seem surprised when the tire tread in the photo didn't match the tires on that car. Next, he strolled across the street and inspected Ellie's Civic. Not a match there, either.

He did note that the back, left tire on Ellie's car was low. He advised her to take it to the nearest gas station or one of Oregon's Les Schwab tire centers before noon.

"What vehicle does your daughter Antonia drive?" Detective Buchanan asked.

"Hey," Trish said. "You leave Antonia out of this. She's having a hard time following the death of her father. And I'm sure her roommate, her RA, or her boyfriend can tell you she hasn't left Portland."

"She drives a Fiat convertible that belonged to my late mother," Ellie said. "It's about four years old."

"I can clear that vehicle without even looking at the tire treads," he said. "I don't want to overstep..."

"There's a first," Trish said.

98

"I don't want to overstep," he repeated. "But, if she were my daughter, I'd get her something more substantial to drive. I've seen those little cars flip on wet pavement. And, they're notorious for breaking down on the side of the freeway. Just saying."

"Thank you for your concern. I'll think about that," Ellie said.

The detective left them standing outside the garage and got in his car to leave.

Trish waited less than a second before speaking.

"Thank you for your concern!" she mimicked. "I'd have put a boot in his rear if he tried to tell me how to raise my child."

"I think I'm in enough trouble here. I think that they think that I might have had something to do with Clarke's death."

"There are too many 'thinks' in that sentence, El. And, that's the cops' problem, too. They're grasping at too many straws."

"Maybe I should swap cars with Antonia during the rainy season," Ellie said.

"I don't think so. If we're going to follow through on our surveillance plans, there's no way you can make that little red convertible blend into the scenery. Your mother chose red?"

"Not everyone in my family is as conservative as I am."

"Agreed," Trish said. "I say, if we want to stake out the nursery to see if the villain returns to the scene of the crime, we definitely have to take my car."

Ellie nodded in agreement.

"Do you think Buchanan has a private life?" Trish asked.

"How would we know?" Ellie answered. To Ellie, the question seemed to come out of the blue.

"He seems to work 24 hours a day."

"Maybe he goes fishing on his days off," Ellie suggested.

"Not much different than his work days," Trish noted. "How many cases do you think he works on at the same time? I mean," Trish added, "is he spending this much time on bank robberies, assaults, and vending machine raids? I'm not down-playing the seriousness of Clarke's death, but it's to the point that a day doesn't seem normal if the good detective doesn't call or stroll up your drive."

"My bet is he delegates the gum machine raids."

FOR THE NEXT three nights, the unauthorized mini-surveillance team parked behind the bank of trees at the nursery. The women had loaded Trish's small SUV with blankets, pillows, flashlights, charged smart phones, and a bag of snacks. They stopped at Wendy's drive-up window each night, and brought along two junior bacon cheeseburgers, some chili, and drinks.

Trish checked her watch by sticking her left arm out the driver's side window and letting the moonlight reflect on the dial.

"You've checked that watch three times already," Ellie said. "And, I'll bet we've been here less than two hours."

"Close. We've been here two hours and twenty-four minutes. Today is Thursday so I'm missing two PBS mysteries on TV."

"True," Ellie said. "But try reminding yourself that you're on an important mission and may solve a real-life mystery."

Ellie wiggled around in her seat. She slipped off her shoes.

"What are you doing?" Trish asked.

"Climbing into the back seat, but I think I'm stuck."

"So is your big toe. In my right ear."

"Sorry. Almost there."

There was an "oomph" as Ellie landed. "I was trying not to open the door and alert anyone that we're out here."

"And?" Trish asked.

"I thought maybe I could see out both sides of the car and the front window from back here, but it's no better. When we were kids, I don't remember cars having these big, hunking headrests on the front seats."

"Does that mean you're making a return flight to the front seat?"

"In a minute. I need to catch my breath. That wasn't one of my more graceful landings."

"Just warn me before you move into my airspace this time," Trish said.

"I'm thinking it might be harder to land with the windshield there."

"Said the mosquito to the fly."

Two more hours passed quietly.

"There must be something we can do to kill time while we wait."

"Don't say 'kill!'" Ellie said.

"I've been meaning to ask you. Do I get a say about who buys your house?"

"It won't be on the market for another month or so," Ellie said.

"It's a shame you spent money re-carpeting the bedrooms."

"Yes and no. Felix has been making noises about having his own room."

The women yawned in unison. Ellie put her shoes back on and yawned again loudly.

"Tomorrow we bring a deck of cards," Trish said.

"This wouldn't be so bad if I didn't have long legs," Ellie said.

"Never—and two more *nevers*—let me hear you complain about having long legs. There's an entire posse of women who would kill for those."

"Don't say 'kill,'" Ellie repeated.

THE FIRST NIGHT of surveillance they each fell asleep and woke up with stiff necks at daylight. The next night they slept in shifts, but neither of them saw nor heard anything suspicious. Two hours before their self-assigned surveillance shift was due to end on Night Three, Trish registered a protest.

"Tomorrow night, we stop at Taco Bell for rations before we head out here," she said.

"You're objecting to another night of burgers?"

"That's affirmative," she said, mimicking Detective Buchanan.

"Fine with me," Ellie said. "I say we head home tonight. I'm cold and I've lost feeling in my toes."

"Do you honestly think that Detective Buchanan and his men would give up this quickly?" Trish asked.

"*What* are you doing? Don't open that door!"

"I heard something," Trish whispered. "I'll be right back."

"Don't you..."

Trish was out of sight within thirty seconds.

Great, Ellie thought. *Why would she do that? Am I supposed to follow her? How many minutes do I give her before I do? What if whoever killed Clarke is out there?*

She reached for the flashlight and discovered Trish had taken it with her. Waiting was killing her. *Oops! There's the "K" word again.*

The car door swung open and Ellie opened her mouth to scream.

"Raccoon," Trish said as she slid in the front seat. "You've got raccoons raiding the outside trash cans."

"I can identify with the raccoons. They're probably scared and hungry out there in the dark," Ellie said.

"Where are the Cheetos?"

"Gone," Ellie said.

"They were here when I left."

"As I said. I can identify with the raccoons."

"How do you suppose a woman stays as thin as Bunny Maguire?" Trish asked.

Ellie surveyed the remains of their evening snacks. The wrappers were now in the floor well of the front seat. "Not by eating like this," she said. "My question is why anyone would name her Bunny. I understand calling the bimbo Bambi, but Bunny has to deal with her name in a professional legal environment."

"So, we give her a code name," Trish said. "The Hare."

"Works for me."

"I like The Hare's sense of humor and her skill in her field. Plus, the interesting way she combines smarts with gutter talk."

"Call me shallow, but I like that The Hare arrives unannounced with cream puffs and chocolate eclairs," Ellie added.

"You do know where she lives, don't you? Our new friend Bunny resides in that fancy-schmancy glassed-in high-rise condo building in downtown Corvallis," Trish said. "You know the one I mean, the sleek one with the wine bar downstairs. The one where a month's lease on a condo is more than anyone we know earns in *three* months."

"Good for her," Ellie said. Then she had second thoughts. "How did Clarke afford his legal fees when she represented him?"

"Who says he'd gotten around to paying the bill before his death?"

"True."

"You don't suppose Bunny has hit men, do you?" Trish asked.

"Nah," they said in unison.

"How did you find the address?" Ellie asked.

"Hardly difficult any more. I did a computer search," Trish confessed. "But, wait. There's more!" She hesitated to catch her breath, then spilled all she had learned. "Bunny doesn't have a formal office. Or *any* office. She arranges all initial contacts with clients in public places or at the client's home."

"She met me at a Starbucks," Ellie recalled.

"She keeps track of billable hours on that tiny calculator 'thingy' she carries. And, she usually takes only high-roller clients or those referred by Legal Aid."

"Representing Clarke must have been a real come-down for her."

"She probably did it as a favor for Bambi."

"I keep wondering, what's the deal with the red soles on Bunny's shoes?" Ellie asked Trish.

"What's the *deal*?" Trish shouted.

Ellie shushed her.

"What's the deal?" Trish whispered. "Can you say Sarah Jessica Parker? Those shoes are designer Christian Louboutin's. They go for $375 a foot. Minimum."

"Oh."

"Louboutins hit the fashion scene the same year Sex and the City washed across TV screens in America."

"So, they're out of date?" Ellie asked. "I find that hard to believe."

"El, Louboutins are *never* out of date."

Trish yawned. "I don't know about you," she said softly, "but the novelty of waiting for something to go 'bump' in the night has worn off for me."

They drove home.

"DOES IT BOTHER you that much of the publicity about Oregon makes the inhabitants sound weird?" Trish asked the next morning.

"Weird or wired?" Ellie asked.

"Well, both since the voters legalized marijuana."

"No. Not particularly," Ellie said. "But, when I was a kid I was impressed about the tales of Oregon's abundant rain. Then, I looked up info about other states when I was in fifth grade and I learned that Hawaii,

Louisiana, Mississippi, Alabama, and even Florida get more annual rainfall than we do."

"Hmmm." Trish appeared to have lost interest in the conversation.

"Those states must have better PR men," Ellie said.

"Oregon's also known for citizens voting by mail and not being allowed to pump their own gas," she added.

"Go back a few years," Trish said, "and you'll remember that the state was also known for welcoming tourists, but then encouraging them to head on back to their home states after spending their tourist dollars here."

"Preferably at a plant nursery," Ellie added.

SHORTLY AFTER MIDNIGHT the next evening at Gardens and Greens, there was a rap on the drivers' side window of the SUV. Both women woke with a start.

The uniformed police officer standing outside the car motioned for Trish to roll the window down.

"Yes?" she asked.

"It's three a.m., Ma'am," he said. "I think we may need to talk."

"Talk?" the women said in unison.

"You two are costing the Police Department a lot of overtime pay by coming out here to sleep. Don't you have beds at home?"

"I beg your pardon," Ellie said.

"Until Detective Buchanan is assured that you two are safe—and not suspects in Mr. Mobley's death—we've been asked to keep you under surveillance."

"Let me get this straight," Trish said. "You're saying that *our* surveillance team is being watched by *your* surveillance team."

"Pretty much, ma'am. We've been assigned to protect you and Mrs. Mobley, while the officers at the detective division determine that you're not in danger. And, frankly, it'd be a lot easier on all of us if you two would stay home at night."

"This isn't a safe thing you've been doing," a second cop chimed in. "And besides, it hampers citizen-police relationships when we have to sit and watch you eat hot chili and fries while all we've got is a thermos of coffee."

"Point taken," Trish said.

"We'll follow you back to make sure you get home safely."

Trish rolled up the window, started the engine and drove back toward the neighborhood from which she and Ellie had come several hours earlier. She knew she'd have to share this story with Harvey. The same man who had been adamant that a 'housewife stake out' wasn't smart would have the last word now. Harvey, who, now that she thought about it, had been growing grouchier by the day...

"AM I THE ONLY one who noticed how young the cops looked last night? That tall one looked like my high school boyfriend," Trish said. "When he was *in* high school."

"I drove away from police headquarters thinking the same thing when Bunny and I met there after Sister Bambi reported Clarke missing."

"I think I'd reword that," Trish said. "It makes Bambi sound like a nun."

Ellie rolled her eyes.

"The cops may have nixed our evening activities, but there's no reason for us to be sitting around here waiting for them to solve the crime. They probably have dozens of crimes they're investigating. We can give this one our full attention."

"They may be short on experience, but we have *no* experience."

"Don't be so sure," Trish said. "We've each lived in the world longer than they have. We knew the victim better than they did. And I bet, if we reviewed the last few months of Clarke's life, we might find something that would help."

A CAR PULLED up in front of Trish's house. If she hadn't seen it through the undraped bay window, the roar of its motor would have alerted her anyway. She'd never heard a car engine before that could roar and purr simultaneously. And, the finish on the chrome!

It wouldn't even need chrome, Trish thought. The shiny black paint beat anything she'd ever seen. *If I die tonight, let me be transported to heaven in that car. Please, God. I'm begging you. A one-way ride.*"

After the initial reaction to the car, Trish met Bunny at the front door calmly.

"Do you have the right house?" she asked the attorney.

"Yes," Bunny answered. She'd swept her long shiny hair over her left shoulder which emphasized her cleavage more than usual.

"I want to talk to you about your friend. You know. The one across the street. The woman who wouldn't even keep a library book past its due date?"

"You've got that right," Trish said. "Ellie won't check out seven-day books because she's afraid the seventh day will fall on a day when the library's closed." Trish hesitated. "She won't even put them through the return slot because she thinks they'll get damaged and she'll get charged for repair."

"That's our girl," Bunny said.

"I assume you're here to talk to me. Solo. Do we need to start with something strong to drink?"

"That's always how I 'need to start' at the end of a work day, but wine will do," Bunny said as she took a seat in the living room.

"You're scaring me," Trish said.

"And, you're conning me. I suspect you don't scare as easily as our friend across the street."

"Nailed it," Trish admitted. She took a seat across the coffee table from Bunny.

"If you two and I are going to form an unstoppable defense team, I need to know what makes the cops' primary suspect tick."

"Ellie?"

"No, the damn cat!" Bunny sipped her wine before speaking again. "Of course, I mean Ellie. Statistics say the spouse is the most likely suspect and—over 75 percent of the time—the guilty party."

"I believe your 'stats,'" Trish said. "But, I don't believe that Ellie killed Clarke."

This conversation was bothering Trish. She was battling between feeling disloyal to Ellie and wanting to help the attorney in any way possible.

"How can I help?" she asked.

"Say this does come to trial, which I doubt," Bunny said. "Will Ellie cave under cross-examination even if she didn't kill Clarke?"

Trish sat quietly, thinking.

"Just your gut level," Bunny said. "I don't need a three-page answer."

"Only if she thought she needed to protect Toni," Trish stated firmly.

"She wouldn't protect you?"

"Why would you ask that? She's my best friend but I wouldn't 'do in' her husband for her."

"Halt!" Bunny yelled. "Remind me not to call you as a character witness. That's just the kind of answer that would get your friend convicted and fried."

"You know this conversation is making me very uncomfortable. First, I don't think we should be talking about Ellie without her here. And, second—or whatever number I'm on—because Ellie didn't kill Clarke. No way. She needs an attorney to protect her if that detective tries to make it look like she's a killer."

"And, that's what I'm going to do," Bunny said in her well-modulated lawyer voice. "The real reason I stopped by tonight was to make sure that you, Ellie and I can work as a team. And, you just proved we can."

"You couldn't have just asked me?"

"No. Not until after I've eaten some of the iced German Chocolate cake I have in the trunk of the car."

"You let gooey baked goods ride in that car?" Trish asked.

"I'm never far from my 'baked goods.' Could you phone Ellie and tell her we'll be there in five minutes? If the three of us are going to crush this investigation, we're going to need all the chocolate and sugar we can digest."

"THAT'S SOME CAR," Ellie said as she opened the front door at the Mobley house.

"Glad you like it. Your ex-husband helped me make the down payment on that baby."

Ellie had often noticed through the years that few Oregonians—other than perhaps smartly-clad business women in downtown Portland—carried their umbrellas routinely. A light-weight trench coat with a hood served most women well as they dashed from home to car to work. Men stored hats in their vehicles as routinely as they carried a spare tire and jack.

Bunny didn't yield to this northwest fashion code. The woman had several brightly colored umbrellas. Today's umbrella brought to mind the drawing on the outside of a Morton's Salt package. Bright yellow with a wooden handle held against a dark navy blue coat... She collapsed the umbrella in one quick motion.

That move must take practice, Ellie thought.

The three women switched from talking about the car to rehashing the case. Bunny's primary interest now, it seemed, was in having company while she downed the chocolate cake.

"HOW TALL DO you think Bunny is?" Ellie asked Trish after the attorney left.

"In her case height doesn't matter. She has what my mother used to call 'presence.' And, according to Mom, when you've got that, every head in the room will turn no matter how tall you are."

"I always look at her shoes," Ellie said.

"That's because you're not a man. Since you asked, though," Trish said, "I'd guess 5' 5" or so. And, with those heels, the sky's the limit."

"Well, I sure had her pegged wrong when Clarke had her on retainer. She's one smart cookie."

"More cake?" Trish offered.

10

"Remind me. Why did you two think that sitting in a car in the dark at the Mobley nursery was a good idea?" Harvey Grover asked.

"Ellie and I don't think the police are *doing* anything," Trish said. "Yet, they told us point blank that Ellie and I are both on their suspect list. Toni, too."

"Not doing anything?" Harvey asked. "They were on hand in the middle of the night to arrest you both for interfering with their investigation."

"Correction. We weren't arrested."

"What was the exact wording they used?" he asked.

"We were 'damned stupid and could have gotten ourselves shot.'"

"And?"

"That we, 'of all people,' should certainly be aware that a murder had occurred on 'this very site,'" she said. "Ellie and I felt that last remark was insensitive, considering Clarke's death and all."

"Go on."

"They said we had three minutes to get the car in gear or get our hands behind our backs for the cuffs. Or something like that."

Harvey assured her that he was as eager as she was that the police remove the two women, along with Antonia Mobley, from a list of murder suspects. "But," he continued, "it won't do any good if you're killed before that happens."

Trish reluctantly agreed that she'd let her husband know in advance of any future "outings" she and Ellie scheduled.

Harvey, though, couldn't let the subject rest.

"Do you know how much we pay in county property taxes each November?" he asked.

Trish recalled the statement that arrived each year between Halloween and Thanksgiving, but she couldn't remember the exact amount.

"I know it goes up annually," she said.

"Exactly. And do you also know that the taxes we pay support public services? Services which, I might add, include police and fire protection?"

"Is this civics lesson necessary?"

"I'm just trying to remind you that you and Ellie do not personally need to solve this crime. We—the two of us and Ellie Mobley—have already paid professionals to investigate crimes."

"Your so-called professionals have Ellie, Toni, and me on *their* suspect list," Trish countered.

"If you two will stay out of their way," Harvey said, "they'll probably have time to clear the three of you and find out what actually happened the night Clarke died."

"Grouch," Trish said under her breath as she left the room.

ELLIE MOVED the afghan and Felix aside gently and pulled herself up from the couch when she heard her cell phone ring. From the volume of the ring, she knew that she must have left the mobile phone in her purse. Now, if she could remember where she'd set the purse when she came in from grocery shopping...

"On top of the refrigerator?" she asked Felix.

She walked into the kitchen and discovered the purse and phone in the suspected place, balanced against a bag of potato chips.

"It's Bunny," Ellie heard when she picked up the call. "You alone or is your sidckick there?"

"Just me and the cat."

"Good. Keep it that way if you can. I'm going to swing by with some additional background questions that have been haunting me. Some of the info I need, you might want to keep private. Even from Trish."

Ellie doubted that. She put the phone down.

"Oh, is Bunny going to be disappointed," Ellie told Felix. "I've got nothing."

What could be so personal that I wouldn't have told Trish? You can't say Bunny isn't thorough. Maybe I'd have come out better in the divorce if she'd been on my side then," she thought. She'd had that thought before, but she had pushed it aside.

Bunny deftly closed her black umbrella and leaned it against the porch railing. Everyone else who walked through that doorway "came inside." Bunny "made an entrance," whether she knew it or not. Today she was wearing a pin-striped skirt and caramel-colored jacket. On anyone else, her attire would have looked like a throwback to women who first began being accepted to law schools in greater numbers in the 1970's. On Bunny, it screamed Northwest Woman with Northeast style.

Bunny carried a simple yellow legal pad of paper in her left hand and a bakery box with a carrot cake in her right hand. Her purse strap hung over her right shoulder, making it tricky to keep the cake from sliding off the cardboard "plate."

"Let me take that," Ellie said.

"Not all of it. I get half."

Ellie guided Bunny toward the kitchen counter, but she suspected that the woman probably knew the house plan by heart now.

"Cake first, questions second," Bunny said. It wasn't a suggestion. It was statement of how the interview would be conducted, and Ellie complied. They swished

118

the cake down with cups of hot tea, and then moved to the living room.

"This won't take long," Bunny said. "But, in case you haven't noticed, I like to be face-to-face when I'm gathering information from clients. It's hard to read people by phone."

"Fine with me," Ellie said. "How can I help?"

"The first thing I need to know is both for my personal information and to defend you against possible accusations of murder."

"I have the feeling we've moved past 'possible,'" Ellie said

"Not until they arrest you," Bunny clarified.

That didn't make Ellie any more at ease.

"Question: Was Clarke Mobley ever abusive to you when you were married to him? Hell, make that 'at any time?'"

The room was quiet. Ellie didn't speak.

"That wasn't the kind of question that most people have to think about before answering," the attorney said.

"True," Ellie agreed. "He was never physically abusive."

"Good. Good for you and good for me. I can stop worrying about anything that might have happened to Bambi during her short but prosperous marriage to the man. And, I can be assured that—if this does come to trial—the prosecutor won't view abuse as a possible cause for you killing the jerk."

119

Bunny hesitated for a minute. "Now describe the degree of verbal abuse and for how many years it lasted."

"After Antonia was born, he treated me like I wasn't as smart as he was. He no longer consulted me about financial decisions and would act surprised if I was more current on world events than he was."

"Yet, the two of you worked side by side at the business?" Bunny asked.

"Yes. And, that probably saved our marriage. Well, until it didn't."

"Go on."

"He never used his how-can-you-be-so-dumb tone when we were around other people."

"Not even around the neighbors? The Grovers?"

"No. But, knowing Trish, she probably sensed that everything over here wasn't roses. And, the verbal assaults weren't so bad that I would have left him. Just belittling."

"Did you sense that most of your acquaintances and work associates liked him?"

"Except when Clarke was drunk," Ellie said. "That was happening more and more this past year."

"That's all I needed to know," Bunny said. "I like to prepare ahead in case a client is later arrested and accused of a crime. And, in this case, I wanted to also make sure that my ditzy sister probably didn't suffer any abuse during their short marriage. Love her as I do, she's not the best at selecting husbands."

Ellie glanced at Bunny's left hand to see if there was a ring.

"You can't always tell that way," said Bunny who missed nothing. "A lot of professional women now elect not to wear wedding rings."

An hour after Bunny Maguire—alias The Hare—left, Ellie realized that Bunny had gleaned all the information she was seeking.

But, I don't know any more about Bunny now than I ever did. So why do I trust her so completely? she asked herself.

THE POTENTIAL SUSPECT list Ellie and Trish had created was longer than either of them would have predicted. They'd been sitting at Trish's kitchen counter for thirty minutes when Ellie sat back and sighed loudly.

"Maybe we should each make our own list of suspects. Then separate the names into an A team and a JV Team," Trish suggested.

"By height and weight?"

"No. Leave all the names on the same list but put a check mark next to the name if the person had *reason* and an *X* if they had opportunity. Then, underline those that had both," Trish said.

"You're sure you couldn't work color-coding into this system somewhere?"

"OK. Cancel all that." Trish started again. "We each make *one* list of suspects in order of most suspicious to the least. Then we combine our lists and discuss each name."

An hour later Ellie was prepared to read the names of her "players." The list Trish made had been ready twenty minutes earlier.

"I'm going to read mine from the bottom to the top," Ellie said. "Like when the high school coaches post the JV team members first so the guys who made that team can be excited about getting to play instead of being disappointed about not making varsity."

"Why would you remember that?"

"Empathy level. It's one of my failings. The last time he was home, Clarke listed my shortcomings as he went out the door. I was too damned empathetic and understanding, he said. There was also a crack about the long length of my legs making it hard for him to buy jeans for me."

"And, those were flaws?"

"That's not important now. I'll read my list. A list that, you'll notice, does *not* include you, Antonia, nor me."

- *Bambi's dog*
- *Bambi's ex-husband*
- *Somebody Bambi hired*
- *Bambi*

"That's it?" Trish asked. "That's what took you an hour to write?"

"Well, I thought of three other people who were mad enough to kill Clarke after the divorce. But I know that you, Antonia, and I didn't do it. What's the point of writing somebody's name down just to draw a line through it a minute later?"

"Gotcha."

Ellie looked pleased.

"Do you want to hear who's on my list so we can then 'combine and narrow?'?" Trish asked.

"Sure."

"Here goes," Trish said.

- *Bambi's Ex*

- *Bunny*

"Why Bunny?" Ellie interrupted. "I thought we decided we like her?"

"Didn't you tell me she claimed over fifty billable hours for legal conferences with Clarke? That's a lot of time to learn to hate the guy," Trish said.

"Agreed. But we obviously know better. Bunny's not the perp," Ellie said. "I'll be quiet. Go on."

- *The husband of a woman Clarke's seeing since marrying Bambi*

"OK," Ellie said. "I can see that as a possibility."

- *Felix*

"Now that's just mean."

- *Anyone who's heard Clarke's deep-sea fishing story three times or more*

"Not Harvey! No!"

"Of course not," Trish said. "But maybe we aren't the only ones who've heard that damn story umpteen times. I've got more on my list," she said and started again.

- *Homer*

"Homer as in *The Odyssey*?"

"Of course not," Trish said. "Don't you call that homeless guy Homer? The one you let sleep in the shed at the nursery on snowy nights?"

"Roamer," Ellie said. "We call him 'Roamer.' And our insurance company would never approve of me letting him stay in the business overnight. It's purely coincidence that the only nights I forget to lock the sheds are snowy ones."

"Shall I go on?" Trish asked.

"You've got more?"

- *One of Clarke's pot-head Colorado customers*

"That'd be a long drive," Ellie noted.

- *A burglar or nocturnal plant thief*
- *A gay man who left the scene in the same state of dress Clarke did*
- *Your new employee Rod*

"Rod never met Clarke," Ellie said. "I think we can take both new employees off the list."

The women were quiet for a minute. "Bambi didn't make your list?" Ellie asked.

"I figured you'd have that market covered," Trish said.

"I did," Ellie said. "How about suicide? Neither of us mentioned that."

"With Clarke's ego?"

"No way," they said in unison.

"Neither one of us listed Santos either," Trish said.

"Because Santos isn't involved. Double 'No way,'" Ellie said. "Sooooo. What *didn't* either one of us know about Clarke?"

"What?" Trish asked. "I'm not sure how to answer that. I'm supposed to tell you what I *don't* know? I assume you're looking for something in addition to the fact that he turned out to be a cad, a cheat and a scumbag. No offense," she added.

"None taken. Was that side there for the twenty-some years that I knew him and I missed it? That makes me question everything about our lives together. And if that's so, what else did I miss? And why am I not sadder? I'm a nice person. I should be sad."

"Here's another 'and,'" Trish said. "*And* is there a part of him that none of us knew—a part that would tell us who killed him?"

"He was just a normal guy," Ellie said.

"I saw a poster once that said, 'Normal is the average of deviance.'"

"I don't think that's helpful right now."

11

The fragrance from the pink Cecile Bruner roses on the trellis outside the "rose house" at the nursery was magical to both adults and children, pulling them from the doorway and beyond, through the rows and rows of roses.

Picturing the roses in full bloom in late spring, Ellie knew it would have been harder to part with the nursery than her home. She looked toward the lattice-sided trellis where the new stock of perennials was partially shaded from bright sunshine. Not a question. She had made the right decision in giving up her home in exchange for keeping Gardens and Greens. She never felt more alive and alert than when she was surrounded by new shipments of spring plants.

While Ellie always greeted the shipments of annuals warmly, her true love was for the perennial plants which burst into bloom in their designated area at the rear of nursery each year. She fell short of *bursting* into song, but she was excited when peonies and hydrangea bushes made their quiet appearances each year. She and other Oregonians also looked forward to the annual shows put on by columbines and butterfly bushes. The butterfly bushes, unfortunately, did so well in the state that they risked being declared "invasive."

Foxglove and veronica, shade-loving plants, were not to be outdone by the hardy geraniums and other sun-loving returnees each year.

A SMALL DECORATIVE box with four chocolate truffles was waiting for Ellie when she arrived at work. She picked it up and looked through the cellophane wrapping. *Who did she know who would spend that much for four candies? Possibly Bunny*, she thought.

"New Hire Rod" walked into the office to let her know that he had arrived for the Saturday shift.

"Did you let anyone into the office?" she asked him. "Who would bring me candy?"

"Most people find that out by reading the card that comes with a gift."

Ellie looked at the desk again. There was a small note card in an envelope where the package had been sitting. "Oops!"

She read silently, then turned to Rod.

"Well, this is a first," she said. "It's a note of apology from the job candidate who didn't show up for his interview."

"Nice."

"The note says he's a single dad with two college-age kids and can't always predict when one of them is going to have control over his schedule."

"Sounds like you could identify with that," Rod said.

"It seems he's enjoyed shopping and browsing here for years and doesn't want to feel uncomfortable about missing the appointment when he comes in for more rose bushes in late spring."

"Do you recognize the name?"

"No," Ellie said, handing the note card to Rod.

"Hey! I know this guy," Rod said. "Unless there are two guys named Steve Evans running around in this part of the state. I coached the guy's twin boys when they were in high school. Great basketball players, those kids were. They could have been awarded scholarships anywhere in the country, but instead they chose to stay close to home."

He turned the note over in his hand. "There's a P.S. on the back. The guy asks if he could buy you a cup of coffee some time."

Ellie reached for the note. "You're making that up!" she said. But, the postscript was there.

"Are you going to contact him?"

"I'm going to share the candies during morning break and not give it another thought," Ellie said.

129

"Big mistake. Steve retired early from the Fire Department after a knee injury. He and his wife had plans to travel while the twins were at University of Oregon, but his wife died before that could happen. He's done a heck of a job raising those two boys since."

"I'm sorry that happened. But it doesn't mean that I plan to call the man."

Rod turned to leave. Then he looked back over his shoulder. "If I'd sent you a box of candy—before I worked here—would you have gone out with me?"

"I'm not ready to go out with anyone," Ellie said firmly.

"Tell me you're not going to be one of those bitter divorced women."

"That ship may have sailed."

"Well, don't take it out on Steve Evans. He's one of the few great guys out there. In addition to me, of course."

"Of course."

"On to other business," Rod said. "Do you want me to readjust the sprinkler timer for warmer weather this weekend?"

"Please. That would have slipped my mind."

"I'm here to serve," he said with a mock salute as he headed out to the yard. "My weekends are yours."

"MOM! WHAT DID YOU DO? How could you?"

It wasn't the greeting Ellie had expected when she picked up the desk phone in the front hallway at home.

"Toni, calm down. I don't know what you're talking about," Ellie said.

"Thackery, of course. The police were here today and interviewed him about Dad's death. They scared the shit out of him."

"Language, Toni. Watch your mouth, please," Ellie said. "I didn't know you two were still dating."

"Well, we aren't *now!* He's scared to death to be seen with me. The cops told him that if he's found to have been anywhere near a crime scene, they can get him deported."

"Toni, that's a little extreme. Don't you think?"

"Mom, do you follow the national news?"

"Well, tell Thackery that I'm sorry that your dad died at an inconvenient time for him."

"Mom!"

"Let's be rational about this, Toni. The police are doing their jobs. They're talking to anyone who has been associated with our family in the past six months to a year."

"Well, they won't have to worry about Thackery being part of our family any more. He broke up with me."

THE PSEUDO-DETECTIVE team of Grover and Mobley met on Thursday morning to review their suspect list.

"I say we cross off the cat. There's no way my sweet Felix could get to the nursery in the middle of the night," Ellie protested.

"We agreed we'd consider every name on the suspect list and only strike a name if we both have solid reason to remove it," Trish said.

"I say we start by eliminating Felix and Bambi's pet. But I repeat myself."

"OK. I'll accept that," Trish said. "Delete 'em. But, we need to find two names of humans we can delete also. It might help if we considered whether it was even possible for a suspect to have been in the area on the night of Clarke's death."

"Repeat after me: access, method, motive," Ellie said. She'd heard Bunny say that the last time they'd talked to the police together.

"I think we can narrow the list down even more if we take the time to talk about each name," Trish repeated.

They agreed to strike new employee Rod Nelson, who had never met Clarke Mobley, off the list. They also agreed that Roamer, who wandered the site regularly, was unlikely to qualify as a suspect.

"See? Progress!" Trish announced.

"Only because if Roamer had wanted to kill Clarke, he would have done it years ago."

They each scanned the list.

Trish yawned.

"Whose idea was it that Clarke was rendezvousing with a gay man that night at the nursery?"

132

Trish sat quietly.

"*Why* would that thought even cross your mind?" Ellie asked.

"His outfit—or lack of one—when he was found?"

"Let's think about this," Ellie said. "Clarke Mobley destroyed our marriage to run off with slutty Bambi. Do you think he'd go to that extreme to hide his true sexual identity?"

"You never know."

"And can't we agree," Ellie said, warming to the topic, "that in twenty-two years of marriage I might have picked up on it if Clarke had even a twinge of interest in meeting gay men?"

"Maybe yes. Or, maybe no. We've established in the past that I'm the worldlier of the two of us," Trish said quietly.

"Are you bringing *that* up again? Give me a break. It wasn't my fault that I didn't know how to tell the little girl kittens from the little boys. Felix was very mature about accepting the name change from Phoebe to Felix. He, by the way, has become very good company since Clarke left."

"I'm happy for you both."

It was quiet for a few minutes. Trish interrupted the silence.

"Think back," she said. "What appealed to you most about Clarke when you first met him?"

"He was so self-assured. In any situation," Ellie said. "For some reason that made me feel loved and protected."

"I can see that."

"And, Clarke was tall and handsome. He looked completely different than he did in later years after he started drinking. The first few years we were married, he'd have a drink or two before we left for a party, and he'd be the life of that party after we got there. *Everyone* invited us—well, Clarke—for that reason."

Ellie stopped for breath.

"Years later he started drinking before dinner every night and was three stops past obnoxious by seven o'clock. Maybe it wasn't *every* night, but often enough that I started turning down invitations without him knowing they'd been extended."

"How do you suppose Bambi dealt with that?"

"No way to tell, but I hope she was prepared for the times he stumbled into the hall closet in the middle of the night thinking he was in the bathroom," Ellie said. "At least she won't have to deal with that any longer."

"Gross."

TRISH AND ELLIE regrouped to, as Trish said, 'examine this case the way true detectives would.'

"I'm hungry," Ellie said before they'd even sat down. "What do your 'true detectives' snack on during their investigations? Do they have these talks while they're driving around or in formal meetings?"

"For all I know they stop for a beer after work and some of their finest work comes after round three."

"Do you think the cops have people on their suspect list that aren't on ours?"

"Ellie, come with me," Trish said.

She tugged her friend's hand and led Ellie into the hallway where a large wood-framed mirror hung.

"You're looking at their prime suspects," she said.

DETECTIVE BUCHANAN phoned at the beginning of the next week to request a time that he could come to Ellie Mobley's house to talk.

"And feel free to invite your friend Mrs. Grover," he said.

"Will do. And my lawyer, Bunny Maguire—whom I believe you've met."

"By all means." *The more the merrier*, he thought as he disconnected the call.

BOTH TRISH AND ELLIE WAITED nervously the morning of the appointment, each eager to hear what was so important that Buchanan couldn't tell Ellie on a land-line telephone connection.

"Maybe it's a trick, and he's coming to arrest me," Ellie said. "And he wants you here to offer supportive platitudes as I'm cuffed, gagged and dragged out to the back seat of a squad car.

135

"Why would a thought like that have crossed your mind?" Trish asked. "By the way, I learned something new about our pal Bunny," Trish said.

"You were checking her references?"

"No. I was eavesdropping at the grocery store. The women in front of me in line—a line that hadn't moved in five minutes while a senior citizen wrote a check instead of using a debit card—were talking about their Zumba class. I don't know how Bunny has time to do it all, but I do now know that she teaches a Zumba class at the racquetball club two nights a week.

"Does the woman ever sleep?"

"Where's Buchanan?" Trish asked.

A quiet knock at the door stopped Ellie from answering.

Ellie ushered the man inside.

Detective Buchanan got right to the point. "We've been working in conjunction with the FBI and the police in Colorado. The folks there have determined beyond a reasonable doubt that Bambi Mobley..."

Trish snickered.

"Yes?"

"Sorry. It's the name. 'Bambi Mobley.' It sounds like 'Namby Pamby,'" she said. "It's the first time I've heard her new name out loud."

"If your friend can contain her mirth," the detective said to Ellie, "I'll continue." He cleared his throat. "Law enforcement agencies in Colorado have determined that the new Mrs. Mobley was in the state of Colorado the night that Clarke Mobley died."

"Damn!"

The detective shot Trish a stern look.

"Does that take Bambi off your suspect list, Detective?" Ellie asked.

"Everyone's still on our suspect list," he said.

The doorbell chimed the arrival of Bunny Maguire, who carried a Dunkin Donuts box.

"Hello all. Hope I haven't missed anything," she said. "Can you share anything else you've learned during your investigation, Detective?"

Buchanan repeated what he'd told Ellie and Trish.

"I thought it was important for you to have this much information in case you and your late husband's new spouse need to confer about burial arrangements or other matters," the detective told Ellie. "I thought it might lessen part of the strain."

"Of course," Ellie said. "Thank you for coming."

The detective nodded to each woman and rose. "I can see myself out," he said.

"Watch the cat," Trish and Bunny said in unison.

"Have I or have I not told you not to talk to the cops without an attorney present?" Bunny asked as she popped a donut hole in her mouth.

"We mostly listened," Ellie said.

"Thin line, my dear. A very thin line."

"Sorry," Ellie said.

"Sorry schmorry," Bunny said. "OK. Fill me in."

"When do we reach the point that I can call 'police harassment' about all these house calls?" Ellie asked.

"Oh, Babe," Bunny said. "You aren't even close yet to having an official harassment complaint. This is 'standard operating procedure' from the cops' point of view."

"If the cops are so smart, why don't they check the security cameras on businesses along the highway? Wouldn't those places still have recordings from that night?" Trish asked. "You can't get to the nursery without going either east or west on the highway."

"That's why your friend here has an attorney," Bunny said. "And, a good one at that. We don't want to ask any questions that we don't know the answers to in advance."

"But we know Ellie wasn't there."

"But, do we know that a car like hers wasn't on the highway?" Bunny asked. "My rule is to defend my client, not to provide leads for the cops."

Trish nodded.

"If I know Buchanan as well as I think I do, he'll get to that in due time. Let's not remind him now."

"Gotcha."

"OUR SUSPECT LIST is going to fit on a 3x5 inch index card pretty soon," Trish said. "They're dropping like flies."

"The cops have an edge on us," Ellie answered. "They can actually interview and interrogate the people they suspect."

"Well, yes, there is that."

"Well, surprise!" Ellie said. "We've got a new lead that dropped right in our laps—or the mail slot at the nursery. I got a statement yesterday afternoon from the company that delivered the cedar mulch."

"How does that help?"

"Both deliveries that arrived here came from the same large outlet that Clarke and I always ordered from in the past. However—and it's a huge however—it looks like the distributor received telephone orders from Clarke in Colorado and didn't realize—or Clarke forgot to tell him— that the delivery address for Clarke's business needs had changed."

"Or Clarke did it on purpose to stick you with the bill," Trish said.

"Sounds like Clarke's kind of thinking, but the theory doesn't hold up," Ellie said. "This was mulch he needed for his grow operation in Colorado."

"OK."

"This company we order from is a huge operation and they sub-contract with mulch businesses clear across the country."

"So, what do we do now?" Trish asked.

"I already did it. I contacted the manager by phone and they told me to keep the mulch they delivered here. He's going to contact Bambi and see if they can 'save the order.' Apparently, it's worth the money to keep their customers happy. He said they'd duplicate the order free of charge for Bambi's Colorado grow site."

Trish was quiet.

"What are you thinking?" Ellie asked.

"I'm thinking that this info will help us re-evaluate our suspects."

"Why?"

"Think about it. It sounds to me like the two deliveries of cedar mulch to Gardens and Greens may not be related to Clarke's death. One load gets misdelivered in Oregon and the company doesn't hear from anybody that an error was made."

"Right."

"The timeline in all this is important. Say Clarke was either sleeping or passed out drunk at your nursery yard the night he died. He's passed out when a truck backs up the driveway and brings the second load that was supposed to go to Colorado."

"You're saying it was an accident that Clarke was buried?"

"I'm suggesting that we think about it as a possibility," Trish said. "I'm also saying that maybe we need to share this information with the cops and let them figure out if it's important."

"The same police who told us to keep out of the investigation?" Ellie asked. "What was the wording? 'We don't want amateurs sullying things.'"

Trish handed the phone to Ellie. "Call them," she said.

"Buchanan was here less than 24 hours ago," Ellie said stalling. "And he pretty much told us to stay out of the way of his investigators."

"Yes. But, you have new information now. You didn't go out 'detecting.' The information came to you."

Ellie walked into the kitchen with the phone in her hand and punched in the non-emergency number for the police department. She knew if she made the call from the living room that Trish would be adding side remarks while she tried to talk to the detective.

She returned less than five minutes later.

"Was he interested?" Trish asked.

"*Interest* might be overstating his reaction. He said he'd make a note of the information. I didn't sense a lot of enthusiasm."

"Don't overthink this," Trish said. "He may have been eating his lunch. The man appears to be over-worked and underfed."

"You're defending Buchanan?"

"Simply giving him a small break. Last time he was here, he looked exhausted."

"I'M HAVING a rough day," Ellie confessed.

"I've been afraid that you might burst if you didn't sit down for a good cry soon," Trish responded.

141

"How can I miss someone I hated during the divorce and detested afterward? How can I grieve for Clarke—the same man I hoped would be struck down by lightening while I was working with the moving company to get all that stuff shipped to Colorado? I wasn't simply annoyed. I genuinely hated the bastard." She paused. "In fact, I still do."

"Strong language for you. How about you're normal after all?" Trish asked. "If you don't let yourself have some mini breakdowns along the way, you'll store up all this negativity and eventually go big time ape shit."

"You been watching Dr. Phil again?" Ellie asked.

"Yes, but the part about the apes was mine."

"I figured as much."

Trish changed the subject: "How are your 'new hires' working?"

"Sheer genius. That's what those 'hires' were. Rod gets three times as much done in a day as Clarke accomplished in a week. And he and the weekday woman, Kristi, put together a free Saturday morning workshop for middle school kids."

"You're kidding me."

"I had my doubts, too. Rod admitted that the first session with the kids was like herding popcorn. The kids arrived for the second session, though, and got right to work. They only meet for three Saturday mornings and they leave each week with a different potted plant and the know-how to keep it alive."

"These kids don't drive, do they?" Trish asked. "And you can't tell me that their parent-chauffeurs don't buy something at the nursery while they're there."

"Well, there is that."

"Genius!"

"Kristi is wrapping the experience into a paper for a Science Education course. Rod's doing it for fun. He's got as much energy as the kids. That's probably why he chose to teach at a middle school."

WHEN SHE WAS TEENAGE, Toni had dreamed of having a garden wedding at the nursery. It had been her private playground during summers. Both she and Harvey Grover often stopped by after their school days. That's when he helped her perfect her softball pitch. Now, Ellie doubted that her daughter would ever visit there again.

The first year they owned the nursery, Clarke had worked evenings for several weeks constructing the white pergolas that were attached on three sides of the sales office. Depending on the season, baskets of orange and variegated geraniums, royal blue forget-me-nots and white daisies, or vibrant petunias put on quite a show. The plants served as "advertising" without a single word needed.

On the shadier side of the building, neon orange and violet impatience intermingled and cascaded from planters which hung from last-century mimics of San Francisco counterculture macramé hangers. This unusual color combination never went out of vogue. It reminded

143

both shoppers and browsers of Oregon's love affair with its fringe hippy population which still flourished in some small coastal communities and the college town of Eugene.

"I NEVER THOUGHT I'd say this, but sometimes I miss hearing a man's perspective on things around the house," Ellie said.

"Felix let you down?" Trish asked.

"No. I'm ready to re-do Clarke's den before I put the house on the market. And I caught myself worrying that my choice in furniture might be too 'girly.'"

"Probably depends on your buyer," Trish said. "Remember, I get veto power before you seal any deal with a new owner."

"I'm hoping the area will pull out of the current real estate slump before I need to sell."

"Meanwhile, back to men..."

"Not you, too," Ellie said.

"Is someone else in your life trying to get you back out there?" Trish asked.

"Rod thinks I should be all google-eyed because one of his friends asked me to coffee."

"And you didn't tell me?"

"It was last week."

"Rod's right."

"I'm not ready," Ellie said. "It was nice, though, to think that there could be life after divorce. That someone would actually want my company..."

"That ass Clarke did a real number on you."

"A little respect, please. I prefer 'that deceased ass Clarke.'"

"Good one!" Trish said. "I knew someday I'd have an impact on you. Speaking of 'impacts,'" she added, "*your* friend Harvey brought a puppy home from the animal shelter. It's a no-kill shelter, but Harvey claims the pup pleaded to be spared."

"I think that's sweet. Were you looking for a pet?"

"Not," Trish said. "Harv was at the shopping mall in south Albany and the folks from Safe Haven Humane Society were showing the 'pets of the week. He claims this one locked eyes with him."

"What kind of dog?"

"The kind with huge feet. I am not thrilled."

"Does it have a name?" Ellie asked.

"I suggested he call her Con Artist but Harvey wants to get to know her before he names her."

"I think it's sweet," Ellie said. "It's so Harvey. Then there's Clarke who tried to convince me to get rid of Felix before the divorce."

Trish gasped.

"Felix and I took care of the problem. We told him the only way the cat was relocating was if we got to dispose of all those disgusting stuffed birds and deer heads," Ellie said. "As it turned out, those were the first things to go in the moving van."

"What sort of person would give away a family pet?"

"I may be jumping to conclusions," Ellie said, "but I suspect the same jerk who'd give away twenty-two years of marriage."

"You can tell Felix for me that he has permission to pee on the bastard's shoes if he returns from the dead and dares step foot in your house."

"Trish!"

"And if the cat won't, I will!"

TWO WEEKS LATER, two men entered the sales office at Gardens and Greens and stood quietly at the front counter.

Ellie recognized Rod, of course. And the customer with him looked vaguely familiar. That happened more and more often with the number of years the nursery had been open. Particularly if the customer paid with cash and she couldn't associate a name from a check or a credit card with the face of a regular customer...

Rod spoke first. "This is your customer and my friend Steve Evans. He's been shopping here for years for the American Rose Society's selections. His neighbors expect to see the new newly-honored rosebush front and center in his yard—along with his distinctive hanging baskets."

"It's nice to meet you," Ellie said.

146

She glared at Rod. "I felt duty-bound to bring him in," Rod said. "With his sons away at college, he's been threatening to put cactus in those hanging baskets so he doesn't have to take over the boys' watering chores this year."

Ellie softened.

"Ignore our friend here," Ellie told Steve. "Let me show you this year's rose. It's one of the few times in recent years that ARS has named a yellow rose. Hybrid tea, of course."

They walked across the nursery yard. Rod gave the man the high sign as soon as Ellie's back was turned.

Later that day, Santos stopped Rod in the yard.

"The man who was walking with Mrs. Mobley in the yard? He's a good guy?"

"One of the best," Rod said.

"OK. Just checking."

"As well we should be. It's up to the two of us to keep her safe from teaming up with another jerk."

Rod and Santos "high-fived."

"Deal," Santos said.

"DID YOU EVER hear anything else about the Great Tire Inspection?" Trish asked Ellie that evening.

"Nope. I'd thought, pretty much, that a tire was a tire now days."

"What scares me is that what you just said made sense to me. When you need to replace the tires on the

147

Civic, remind me to lend you Harvey for a couple of hours. He's a man who lives to buy tires and hand tools." She hesitated for a minute. "I wasn't sure the tire exam made any sense, but Bunny predicted Clarke's killer would turn out to be someone who knew him. I've been thinking about that."

"Careful," Ellie said. "That could be you or me."

"That would leave *you*. We both know that I can't keep a secret."

12

Ed Buchanan sat down with his colleague Lt. Jill Andersson. The young lieutenant hadn't been on the force long, but Buchanan respected her thoroughness on past cases and her ability to chase down every possible lead. Recently, she had solved a case by following a thread of evidence that he thought was far-fetched at best.

"Do we know how the deceased got to the nursery?" the young lieutenant asked.

"We're assuming in one of the Gardens and Greens vehicles."

"Okay-ee," she said, dragging out the word to three syllables. "He may have gotten to the pub up the road that way, but how did he *arrive* at the nursery?"

"Damn! We don't know! I love it when you're right."

"I'll call the taxi companies," Andersson said.

"I'll check with the airport shuttle guys."

"At least they keep records. Local taxi drivers—and the same probably goes for Uber—appear to just drive and charge."

"And hold out their hand for the tip," Buchanan added.

ELLIE WAS SURPRISED to hear Steve Evans' voice when she picked up the home phone. It was his ever-so-slight southern accent that tipped her.

"I've been thinking. Maybe I was out of line in asking you out for coffee."

"No," Ellie said. "There was nothing wrong with your invitation. That was my fault. I'm still learning how to be divorced."

"Tell me about it. They ought to offer Widower 101 at community colleges."

Ellie took a deep breath. "Do you have plans for tonight?" she asked.

"Like right now? I'm not sure. How about you?"

"I plan to be at Panera's Bread in Corvallis in half an hour."

There was only a slight hesitation.

"Now isn't that a coincidence!" the man said. "I'm thinking quarter to eight."

"See you there."

What have I done? Ellie thought as she walked into the bedroom to change her top.

ELLIE PULLED INTO the parking lot in front of the bakery-soup shop. She recognized customer Steve Evans seated at an outdoor table. He had a black scottie dog at his feet.

"My dog, Maggie, and I've decided it may be too cold to sit out here after all," he said. "We're glad you came."

"Me too," Ellie said. "Can Maggie go inside with us?"

"We'll find out," he said as he stood and picked up the dog's leash.

They walked inside and to the very back of the bakery where they found a small table away from the other diners. No one seemed to notice Maggie nor object.

"I brought the dog in case we run out of conversation," Steve admitted.

"Well played," Ellie said. "This getting-out-in-the-world-again stuff isn't easy, is it?"

They ordered soup and rolls and Steve produced a couple of dog treats from his coat pocket for Maggie.

They visited for almost forty minutes with no awkward pauses.

"Maybe we could do this again sometime?" Steve asked. "Depending on your schedule and Maggie's?"

"That'd be nice," Ellie said. "But please don't be offended if I have to beg off sometimes."

Darn, she thought. That makes it sound like more than he intended. "There are nights when I come home from work totally wiped out," she added.

"I hear you," he said. "This dating thing isn't easy when you're a grown up. But I'll call. And, call again if it doesn't work the first time."

"Great."

ELLIE DIDN'T HAVE time to remove her coat on arrival at the nursery before Rod appeared at the office door.

"Steve says you met him for coffee," Rod said.

"This employer/employee relationship is getting out of whack," Ellie answered. "You and Steve have been talking about me?"

"I'm just looking out for you."

"Rod, could I ask you something?"

"Anything at all." he said.

"Have you gone out with anyone since your divorce?" Ellie asked.

"I'm not there yet."

"So, work on it!" she said. "And I mean that in the most motherly, non-interfering-boss-lady way."

"Gotcha."

"YOU HAD A DATE and you didn't tell me?" Trish squealed.

"It wasn't exactly a date. But it was a pleasant hour chatting with a new friend."

"You sound like a character in a 1940s novel," Trish said. "Spill!"

"It was just nice to know that someone might like my company and would *choose* to spend some time with me."

"I always have," Trish said.

"You know what I mean. If I *did* want the company of a man, it'd be a possibility."

"That shit Clarke really did a number on you. But, I repeat myself."

"And, once again, that will cost you ten cents in the Swearing Jar," Ellie said. The Swearing Jar hadn't sat on Ellie's kitchen counter since Toni left home, but she was sure she could find it on a shelf in one of the kitchen cupboards. Surely Clarke wouldn't have taken that.

FELIX WAS BASKING in the sun that shone through the dining room window. Ellie, who hadn't seen or heard him leap onto the dining room table, walked across the room and lifted the cat.

"You know better," she said. As she sat down on the couch, she pulled the cat onto her lap and began to lightly massage the muscles in his upper back.

The cat stretched with pleasure and settled in for a nap on her lap.

153

"Soft life you've got, cat," Ellie said. "If you could talk, maybe you could help me figure out what happened to the other guy. The one who insisted on throwing you out in the rain instead of having an indoor litter box. Remember him? Big guy who stepped on your paws if you weren't careful?"

The cat ignored the question. Ellie wished she could do that with the phone message that had been left by Bambi Mobley this afternoon while Felix was the only one home. It had given Ellie a start when she heard the woman's voice on the answering machine.

She'd forgotten how much she hated that voice. It was like getting a taped message from Dora the Explorer. Squeaky but know-it-all and pushy at the same time. She couldn't simply ignore the call, because there was obviously a new problem concerning Clarke's death.

Bambi Mobley's message said she was fighting to halt the autopsy that had been requested jointly by the coroner and the police department to determine the cause of death for Clarke E. Mobley. And, Bambi wanted Ellie to join in putting a stop to the procedure.

After listening to the shrill message twice, Ellie turned to the internet to find out if autopsies were done every time there was a suspicious death. She also wanted to know if the "ex-spouse" even had a right to protest.

An hour later, she knew more than she'd ever wanted to know about an "evidentiary autopsy" and the medical procedures used to perform the examinations.

"What do you say we call Trish?" she asked Felix. She'd already decided not to contact Antonia, who didn't need to lose sleep and study time by being pulled into this drama. If the police requested an autopsy, Ellie thought, there was little anyone could do to prevent it.

It did put anyone who was a suspect in the death in an awkward position, she reasoned. If you were guilty of murder, you probably wouldn't want evidence of your involvement to turn up during an autopsy. And if you weren't guilty but had loved the guy, it would be hard to approve the invasive procedure which—in layman's terms—amounted to slicing and dicing. Which camp did Bambi fall in?

ELLIE SMELLED the chocolate chip cookies before Trish was all the way through the front door.

"Are you intentionally trying to fatten me up?" she asked.

"No. We both know I only bake when I'm bored, when I'm alone, when I have company, when the weather is bad, and when it's sunny."

"Which is it today?"

"All of the above. The TV news guy predicts sun with intermittent showers and possible clearing later tonight. Harv is asleep in his chair in front of the TV, which makes it difficult to decide whether I'm alone or have company," Trish said. "Cookies anyone?" she asked. "I had to take them with me to make sure Harv and Super Dog didn't eat them all."

"Does the puppy have a name yet?"

"We both know Harv's an old softy. He named her Mary—after his mom."

"YOU HAVEN'T RETURNED Bambi's call?" Trish asked.

"Not yet. I wanted to have more information. I'd have assumed it would be Bambi's decision whether to have an autopsy or not. She was the 'wife in residence' at the time of Clarke's death."

"Wife in residence?" Trish asked. "How about 'whore at home'?"

"You're terrible, but I like it." Ellie grabbed another cookie. "I haven't called Bambi..."

"I prefer 'Bimbi.'"

"Stop," Ellie said. "I want to talk seriously for a minute to make sure you think I'm doing the right thing by not returning her call. According to what I read today..."

"And, we all know how accurate the internet is."

"...the family has to be notified. That's Bambi, in this case."

"Family? She *barely* knew the guy," Trish said.

"Good one. But, please, be serious for a minute. Apparently, most state statutes authorize autopsies to determine the cause of sudden, suspicious, or violent deaths."

"Closed case," Trish said. "It sounds to me like Clarke's death qualifies on all three counts. So why would

Bambi protest?" She passed the cookie platter back to Ellie.

"I can think of all kinds of reasons. But, then, I've been mulling this all afternoon."

"I'm sure you have."

"For starters, maybe Bambi thinks an autopsy will show drug use," Ellie said. "Or, maybe she simply can't stand the thought of it."

"Maybe he'd already left her," Trish said. "And I can think of one more 'maybe.' I still think she killed him. Or at least arranged for it to happen."

"Well, it's a murder investigation so the police call the shots..."

"Poor choice of words," Trish said.

"We don't even know why Clarke was in Oregon instead of Colorado. I kept track of him for over twenty years," Ellie said, "and Bambi misplaced him within two months."

"Bambi definitely stays on our suspect list."

"I THINK I FIGURED out what's going on with Harvey," Trish said.

"The moodiness? You said he'd been grouchy."

"A little less so since Mary's tagging along wherever he goes."

"Good," Ellie said.

"Yeah. He mentioned last night that his dad died during Harv's freshman year of college. I think Clarke's death brought back some of the memories Harvey thought he'd buried."

"I don't think I've ever heard about his dad's death," Ellie said.

"The man owned a logging operation. He died when a tree the crew was falling took a bad bounce when it hit the ground."

"That's terrible."

"Like I said, Clarke's death may have brought some of those memories back. Harv and his sister made a trip with their dad late in the summer before Harv's freshman year of college."

"That's an empathetic guy you've got there," Ellie said. "And, for the record, I see that as a good quality."

"He's worried about Toni."

"IS THAT A BAG of chocolate kisses in your hand?"

"How did you tell that from fifteen feet away?" Trish asked as she came up the driveway to Ellie's home.

"My detecting skills?" Ellie said. "Which reminds me... As I was going to sleep last night I had this epiphany."

"I can't even spell 'epiphany.'"

"Trish, I think we may have messed up big time as detectives. We keep talking about suspects, but we've never concentrated on motive. Motive, Trish," Ellie said. "If we can figure out *why* someone—other than me, of course—would want to kill Clarke, we might have our guilty party."

"I wish I'd said that."

"Doesn't matter. Now that we've thought of it, let's go the next step and figure out *why* someone other than me wished him ill."

"'Wished him ill?' Have you been reading Victorian novels again?"

"No, but I try to watch my mouth, so I don't slip and say something evil in front of Toni. Like 'wanted to rip his lying heart out of his chest, ventricle by ventricle...'"

"Wise woman," Trish agreed.

"I'll get the legal pad."

"Is there some reason we always have to start with that stupid pad of paper?"

"It makes me feel official," Ellie said.

"Fine. Get the paper. Then write 'business deal gone bad' followed by 'gambling debt' as numbers one and two for motive."

"Ooh! You're good at this."

"I wasn't as close to the victim as you were," Trish said. "Thank Gawd," she said under her breath.

"I heard that," Ellie said as she came back into the living room. "Trust me, there isn't a day that goes by that I don't wish I'd run like heck the first time I met Clarke."

"Where did you meet?"

"You have to promise not to laugh." Ellie hesitated. "At a church picnic."

Trish whooped.

"You laughed!"

"That wasn't a laugh. That was my war whoop signaling that I'm ready to get down to business. If we have established a likely motive, it will be easier to figure out who might have killed the bastard."

"So, I can send a thank you note?"

"No" Trish answered. "So, Antonia doesn't have to go through life not knowing what really happened to her dad."

"Gotcha. It sounds much more noble when you put it that way," Ellie agreed. "What were those first two motives you had earlier?"

THE POSSIBLE MOTIVES were neatly written on the lined yellow tablet page:

- *Money*

- *Jealousy*

"Wait! That would be me," Ellie objected. "I can tell you right now. That didn't happen." She hesitated. "But, if I'd known everything then that I know now, it might have happened. Does that count?"

"Strike the previous Number Two," Trish said.

- *He couldn't keep up with Bambi in bed and died of exhaustion.*

- *He got a bad diagnosis from his doc and was too chicken-shit to deal with it.*

"So you think Clarke hired someone to kill him?" Ellie asked. "Oh, I don't think so. Clarke wasn't that brave. Even on a good day."

"Don't question these. Just 'let the ideas roll,' as they say. We can edit the list later," Trish reminded her. "It's called 'brainstorming.'"

• *Homesickness*

"That's a stretch."

"Do you want me to brainstorm or not?" Trish asked. "My brain works more in 'slight showers' than 'major storms.'"

"Continue."

• *Humiliation among extended family*

• *Hatred*

"Can we stop at ten or do we need more?" Ellie asked.

"A zillion. We don't want to miss a single possible motive."

• *As Johnny Cash sang, somebody did it 'just to watch him die.'"*

"I loved him. I thought we were happy," Ellie said. "But, I repeat myself."

"Perfect! If that's the case, then you, my dear, had no motive!"

13

"My pal Steve looked a little down when I saw him the other day," Rod told Ellie. "What'd you do? Break his heart?"

"No. I explained my work schedule here and turned down a chance to tour the rose gardens at his house."

"Idiot."

"I beg your pardon?" Ellie asked.

"Gardens and Greens has been supplying the guy with nursery stock for probably fifteen to twenty years and you won't even take the time to tour the man's garden? It's his pride and joy."

"If you haven't noticed—and it's none of your business to notice—I plan to distance myself from men."

"Big mistake!" Steve said.

"You're giving divorce advice?"

163

"I'm more qualified than most," he said. "Steve's a good guy. That's all."

"Thank you, Dear Abner."

NOT HEARING FROM the police made Ellie uncomfortable. Did that mean they'd abandoned their investigation or were they waiting for results from the autopsy?

Detective Edward Buchanan notified Ellie late that night that he and the police chaplain would be stopping by her home the next morning to give her some new information. He suggested that she might want to have a family member present during the visit.

After some thought, she decided that she could relay anything the detective had to tell her to Toni after the visit. She was straining to give Toni as normal a freshman year as possible under the circumstances. Toni, in turn, was striving to be as hard to like as possible lately.

Ellie called Trish and the two of them greeted the men the next morning, then watched as the detective and his guest walked across the room and selected opposite ends of the living room couch to be seated.

The women took their seats across the room and waited for Detective Buchanan to speak first.

His meeting, his agenda, Ellie thought.

"We have some additional information about your ex-husband's death, Ms. Mobley."

"I see."

"This puts a little different light on things. That's why I asked the chaplain to join us this morning."

"You don't suppose you could just blurt this out, do you?" Trish asked as Ellie left the room to get four ceramic mugs and the coffee pot. The men didn't speak again until Ellie returned.

"The news the detective has to share with you doesn't lessen your loss, Ms. Mobley," the chaplain said, "but it may help you carry the sorrow."

"Right," the detective said. "The coroner has now determined that Clarke Mobley could have expired before he was buried in the mulch."

Both women stared at him.

"Then how did he die?" Trish asked.

"Combining the facts that you two provided with those gleaned during our department's investigation on site the night of his death—with the medical information that the coroner gathered—we now believe he either fell or sustained a blow to the head *before* the mulch was delivered," Buchanan said.

He took a breath.

"The night the victim died," Buchanan continued, "we found blood evidence on one of the low garden statues in the area. We've now confirmed that it was your husband's blood. We found his shirt, underwear, socks, and pants a short distance from the pile of mulch that covered him. There was no blood on the clothing."

"And?"

"His wallet was intact with identification and less than twenty dollars inside. The wallet was in the pocket of the pants."

Ellie took a sip of the coffee as she worked to absorb the information.

"Do you remember how cold it was that morning at the nursery?" Buchanan asked. "It had to be below freezing during the night. I'm puzzled by the thought of a victim out running naked through the countryside at that hour in that temperature."

No one responded.

"We now think the victim must have been moving through the nursery yard on foot. Well, in boots, anyway," Buchanan corrected himself. "And maybe carrying his clothes. There were many of his footprints—er, boot prints—in the general area of the mulch pile."

"It's not like he didn't have appropriate clothing," Ellie said. "He bought a leather jacket with a fleece collar maybe six months before he left Oregon."

"What else have you confirmed?" Trish asked the detective.

"The victim had multiple bruises on his body, but the coroner suspects those are more likely the result of a full fall than from being pummeled in a fist fight. But, it could be either. None of us was present. Or, at least I assume that to be true," Buchanan said.

Trish looked like she was going to speak, but Ellie gave her "the look." The same look that mothers across the country give their children to silence them in church or when visiting at a nosy neighbor's house.

"The lab guys suspect that the deceased was unconscious, but not yet expired, when the mulch was delivered and deposited. They suspect he may have been asleep or passed out on the ground. There was some bruising to the left side of his face which could have come from a fall to the ground or—equally possible—from combat with a right-handed combatant."

Buchanan took a breath and continued.

"The weight and quantity of the mulch could have knocked him to the ground or, as we know, covered and crushed him after he was already prone. Whether he was already unconscious, had fallen and was unable to get up—or was knocked to the ground as the truck driver backed up and released the load—is still a question.

"One thing's for sure. It wouldn't have mattered how fast we dug that morning. His lungs collapsed within seconds under the weight of the mulch on top of him," Buchanan summarized.

"So, you're here to tell us you don't really know much more than you did before the autopsy?" Trish asked.

Ellie shot her "the look" again.

"No," Buchanan said patiently. "We're telling you he wasn't shot, wasn't strangled, wasn't run over by a tank, wasn't stabbed through the heart, didn't take a bullet, hadn't consumed rat poison, wasn't hit in the crosswalk and thrown onto the property..."

"I see."

"He died of suffocation and injuries caused by the weight of the mulch," Buchanan summarized.

The chaplain interrupted. "He's saying that death was quick and that the cause of death remains under investigation. For many of us, it's helpful to know that the victim didn't suffer at length."

As opposed to his first wife and daughter, Trish thought.

"And?" Trish asked aloud.

"As I said, the information you two provided helped us. We've confirmed that the company that delivers mulch instructs its drivers to back into driveways that are located off main highways. It's a safety precaution so their drivers don't have to later back onto a busy highway after the delivery."

It was the detective's turn to sip his coffee. He took his time, then spoke again.

"It's entirely possible that the driver released the load of mulch that early morning without ever seeing the body—dead or alive," Buchanan said.

"One other thing," Buchanan added. "The lab tests also showed that the victim had alcohol in his system. Well above the legal limit for drunk driving. The tests also indicate marijuana use within fourteen days of his death. That, of course, could reflect either the Oregon or Colorado lifestyle."

"You're just a fountain of information today," Trish said.

"While these details may or may not be comforting," Buchanan continued, "they don't point us in a definite direction to determine whether he was pushed to the ground or tripped on his own. It still leaves us to determine whether he was the victim of an accident or a murder."

"You're not thinking 'natural causes'?" Trish asked.

"Negative."

Ellie sat quietly, taking in the news and pondering whether it made any difference. "Which way are you leaning, Detective?" she asked.

"Frankly, I was hoping one of you might have the answer."

"Sir," Ellie said to the chaplain. "Do you come along on all these house calls?"

"I do," he said. "Not all widows or widowers have the support that you appear to have from your friend here. No one should be alone at a time like this."

Ellie stood. "I want to thank you both for coming," she said. "I'm going to drive to the university and give this news to my daughter."

"Can you let me know when you've communicated with her?" Buchanan asked. "I'll hold up on releasing any details to the press until after you've talked with her."

"Absolutely," Ellie said.

"Speech pattern," Buchanan said under his breath. He'd thought that the first night he'd met Ms. Mobley. "And, there's one other thing. I'm asking that you and your daughter not leave the state until further notice."

"Where would we go? Toni's headed toward final exam week and I have a business to run."

"I want to make sure you understood me. I'm telling you *not* to leave the state while you're both being investigated for murder."

"Oh."

"And, we're reminding *you* not to talk to Antonia or Ellie without their attorney present," Trish said.

Buchanan ignored the remark.

"Perhaps you, Mrs. Mobley, would prefer that I call your daughter?"

Ellie hesitated. "Antonia might respond better to you," she said, "but I'm her mother and I need to do this. Even if I get a sour response."

"She sounds like a normal college freshman," Buchanan said. "It'll get better. By junior year, she may even respect you again."

"One can only hope," Ellie said. "I'll contact her this afternoon."

"Thank you."

"WHAT A WARM and wonderful friendship those two seem to have," the chaplain said as he got back in the car. "They're like bread and butter. Or salt and pepper."

"Or drunk and disorderly," Buchanan said under his breath.

"Sugar and spice," the chaplain countered.

"Aid and abet."

TRISH WAS THE FIRST to speak after the men went out the door. "I'm having a hard time believing what I just heard," she said. "When I walked across the street to your place, I thought I was going to hear that the police had arrested someone on suspicion of murder."

"Far from it. You heard Buchanan. He ordered Antonia and me not to leave the state."

"Not good," Trish said. "He makes it sound like you and Toni have spots number one and two on *his* suspect list."

"This is a nightmare."

"Speaking of nightmares," Trish said, trying to lighten the mood.

"Yes?"

"I'm not sure about Toni at age eighteen, but I'd bet that black and white horizontal stripes won't be your best look."

"Thank you."

ELLIE ARRANGED to meet Toni on campus and then picked up Trish to ride shotgun on the drive to Portland.

She wasn't as concerned about telling her daughter that she couldn't leave the state as she was about passing on the latest info about Clarke's death. She hadn't mentioned to Toni earlier that her father had been found "in a state of undress," as the police report said. Now she knew she had to give her daughter all the sordid details before the facts appeared in the newspaper.

171

"GROSS," Toni said, when she heard more details of her father's death.

Ellie was left speechless by her daughter's reaction.

"Let's not judge," Trish said. "Maybe he had been sleeping under a blanket in the office and thought he heard something in the nursery yard."

"Thanks, Trish," Toni said. "Nice try and all that, but I'm not buying it."

"These facts don't change that we lost Dad," Ellie said quietly. "I didn't want you to be shocked if all this information becomes public."

"You should have told me that earlier," Toni said. "He was my father."

"You're right. And I was wrong."

"What else have you left out, Mom?" her daughter asked.

"Nothing that I know of."

Except for that criticism, Toni listened to the new information calmly. That worried Ellie more than if her daughter had wailed and carried on about the unfairness of it all. The three women agreed that the best thing that could happen now was that the crime reporter at *The Oregonian* would be home with acute bronchitis and miss reporting this follow-up story.

"PARDON ME for being ghoulish," Trish said as Ellie steered the car up the on-ramp to Interstate 5 South.

172

"But does this information help us narrow down our suspect list? Do we assume Clarke tripped and fell or was pushed?"

"The first thing that went through my mind," Ellie said, "was that Santos and I moved some of the garden statues and birdbaths after Clarke left for Colorado. That would mean Clarke could have tripped in the dark. But either way…"

"He had no business being at the nursery," Trish finished. "Naked."

"Precisely."

"Do you realize that your first reaction was to take the blame for him possibly falling? When a husband screws up—even an ex-husband—it's not automatically your fault."

"You're right of course," Ellie said. "I did that a lot when I was married to him."

"Do you suppose he planned to steal something?" Trish asked. "Maybe you need to count the shovels."

A phone rang in the car and Ellie reached across the seat to the passenger side floor in an effort to retrieve her purse.

"That's it. I'm taking you by the Honda place so you can talk 'hands free," Trish said.

Trish reached for the purse and retrieved the phone. She answered and heard Toni's voice.

"Everything OK?" Trish asked automatically.

"You and Mom have been playing together too long," Toni protested. "Tell you what. If there's ever a time when things aren't OK, I'll text you."

"Yeah, yeah," Trish answered. "Your mom's driving. Can I deliver a message to her or do you want me to hold the phone to her ear?"

"I think the State Police would call that 'skirting' the no call/no text law for drivers. I called because I'd like to be able to concentrate on classes instead of worrying about the police showing up here again. So, I was thinking. Why couldn't you, Mom, and I request to take lie detector tests?"

"Interesting thought."

Trish repeated the idea to Ellie.

"I don't think so," Ellie said vaguely. "On the cop shows on TV, the lawyers object to the suspect taking a lie detector test."

Toni, who could hear the response through the phone, groaned. "Mom, I don't think we should rely on TV dialogue writers for our legal advice. You can't be serious."

"That was just my immediate reaction," Ellie said. "I'll give it some thought. In the meantime, Trish and I are working on a suspect list and have set aside time this afternoon to narrow that list."

"You're willing to play junior detective, but you question taking a scientific test to clear yourself as a suspect, Mom?"

"I said I'd think on it, Toni. And while I'm doing that, maybe you can push all this stuff to the back of your mind."

"Yeah. Sure thing," Toni said sarcastically, and the line went dead.

"Do we have time to stop for lunch or is Harvey expecting you home?" Ellie asked.

"Harv is golfing today. Unless there's been an overnight improvement in his swing, he'll be on the course a long time."

TRISH SPOKE FIRST after the waitress delivered the cheeseburgers and extra home fries.

"Do you think Harvey and Clarke were close?"

"Once, maybe, but not so much after Clarke started chasing Bambi—and who knows who before her," Ellie said. "Maybe your guy's grieving the friendship they used to have."

"That's a little deep for Harv. He's a man. He's probably worrying that his number is coming up next. I told him that if God truly calls up people in alphabetical order, He already gave Harv a pass this round. Grover comes before Mobley."

"That's terrible, but it reminds me," Ellie said. "I brought home the forms to change back to my maiden name, but I haven't filled them out yet."

"Changing your mind?"

"Not."

"Then, what's the holdup?"

"There are a couple of things," Ellie answered. "Toni thinks that changing my name is 'disrespecting' her dad."

"If she wants to talk about disrespectful behavior toward her parents, you're not first in line."

"Well said. The other hang-up, though, is whether to use my maiden name or go back a generation and honor my grandparents by using their name. I was close to them when I was young."

"Your maiden name was Michaels. Right?"

"How did you remember that?"

"No idea. Some days I can't remember if I ate breakfast and other days I can recite the entire Gettysburg Address," Trish said. "What was your grandparents' last name?"

"Schinnheimer."

"Have you lost your mind? Go with Michaels and you won't have to change your initials."

"There's a short waiting period after I file the paperwork anyway."

"Not for us," Trish said. "Let's try it out for size."

"What?"

"Hello, I'm Trish Grover," Trish said, extending her arm across the restaurant table. "Pleased to meet you, Ms. Michaels."

"Why, thank you. I think we'd better finish our lunch and head back to the Michaels estate."

"DOOR'S OPEN," Ellie called when she heard the knock. She assumed it was Trish at this hour.

"Not a good idea," a male voice answered.

Ellie walked across the room and looked through the peephole in the front entry door. Harvey stood there looking uneasy. What was that, she wondered.

When she swung the door open, a small furry object attached itself to Ellie's right fuzzy pink slipper.

"Well, come on in," she said. "And, bring your little cannibal with you." It was the first time Ellie had seen who she assumed was the notorious young Mary—labeled Canine the Cute by Trish who had quickly gotten attached to the pup.

Harvey Grover scooped the dog up in his arms and stepped inside. He turned down the cup of coffee that Ellie offered, but took a seat and pulled the pup in closely under his right arm. "She's kind of a handful at this age," he confessed.

"It gets better," Ellie said. "I used to say the same thing about Antonia."

"That's what I came to talk to you about. How's Toni doing?"

"She has good days and bad days since Clarke died," Ellie said. "The bad days seem to be getting farther apart."

"That's good. I wondered if you'd mind if I took Canine Incorrigible here up to Portland to see Toni. I thought it might cheer her up."

"Wonderful idea!" Ellie exclaimed. "I'd recommend calling Toni ahead of time to see if her class load is lighter one day or another."

"Maybe we could go by a casual restaurant with outside seating for lunch. I don't think the county health inspectors would appreciate having Mary inside most eateries."

Only Harvey would say 'eatery,' Ellie thought.

"Great idea," she said aloud. "It's early in the term so Toni shouldn't be too bogged down with coursework right now."

"Right," Harv said. He looked down at Mary who had now snagged a magazine off a low table next to the chair. "Sorry," he said. "What was that we used to say about bratty kids? Oh, yeah. 'She's precocious.'"

"She's precious," Ellie corrected.

"Hold that thought while we go out the front door," Harvey said. He corralled Mary in his arms and stepped outside.

14

Detective Buchanan walked up the stone driveway at Ellie's home, stopping to admire the new petunia starts that filled the bed between the front lawn and the driveway. He hadn't called ahead this time. He felt it would be to his advantage to catch the "lady of the house" off guard.

Trish had seen a police car cruise up the street, and immediately called Ellie and Bunny.

"Bunco!" Trish yelled. "Are you expecting a cop car?"

"Good grief, no. Nobody's called. I'm in my shorts and an old T-shirt."

Both women heard the doorbell ring—Trish through the phone connection and Ellie three feet from where she was standing.

"Damn," Ellie said. "You're right. Can you get over here?"

"On my way."

ELLIE STEPPED to the door and let Detective Ed Buchanan in the house.

"I'm sorry to surprise you, Ms. Mobley," he said.

Ellie didn't think he sounded sorry at all. "You got the 'Ms.' part right this time, but I've filed to change my last name."

"Why would you do that?"

"My husband, well, late husband, and I were divorced. I don't wish to be associated with that name any longer. Particularly after all the local news coverage of his death." She hesitated before adding, "Also, there's another Mrs. Mobley now."

Trish let herself in while the detective and Ellie pulled out chairs at the dining room table.

Bunny came in right behind Trish, announcing that she just happened to be in the neighborhood. (After receiving Trish's phone call, that is.)

Attorney Maguire was prepared, as always, for the day's freezing weather. She wore leather pants below a creamy cashmere turtle neck sweater and a lambs' wool open vest. She looked like a million dollars, but she didn't think twice about flopping down on the sale-priced area rug near the fireplace in Ellie's living room. She soaked in the heat for a few minutes, then joined the others at the table.

"Detective Buchanan," Trish said. "I'd like to introduce you to the future Ms. Michaels."

"You just drew a name out of a hat?" he asked Ellie.

"No. It was my maiden name. By the first of the month, if the judge has time to sign the order, I'll be Elizabeth, or Ellie, Michaels again."

"How does your daughter feel about this?"

"She's OK with it," Ellie said.

"Are we just chatting here, or is that an official police inquiry?" Trish asked pointedly as she sat down at the table.

"There will be no 'chatting' unless the detective here wants to exchange recipes," Bunny said pointedly.

The detective looked uncomfortable. "I'm here for an official reason," he said. "I was hoping to talk to the ex-wife of the deceased. Alone. Do you three spend all of your time together?"

"If you haven't noticed, this is a neighborhood where we all watch out for each other," Ellie said. "Isn't it the police department that sponsors Neighborhood Watch programs?" (Never mind that she'd cursed the neighbors who'd had their noses to the front windows on the day the moving van had arrived at her house.)

"Well, yes," Buchanan said. "But I'd like to tour the house with the former wife of the deceased without anyone interrupting our conversation or distracting us."

"You'll need to have a search warrant," Bunny said. "Unless, that is, Ellie gives you permission."

"All citizens are welcome to have an attorney present," the detective said curtly. "But maybe you could wait until I have time to tell you what I'm looking for before you object to my visit."

"Shoot," Bunny said.

"That's the last thing I plan to do. I want to walk through the house, room by room, trying to get a feel for the deceased's former lifestyle."

"In that case," Ellie said, "this is the living room." She pointed toward the end of the room. "You'll notice it's an open floor plan, leading directly into the dining room and an inefficient aisle kitchen with too little counter space for two cooks to work at the same time."

"Why do I suspect that you never sold real estate?" he asked.

Trish and Bunny tagged along as they toured the three bedrooms and two small bathrooms. The detective lingered in the hallway where framed family photos hung, but otherwise moved right along.

When they returned to the living room, Ellie took a deep breath and spoke first. "Now, why don't you take a seat, Detective, and tell me what you were truly looking for."

"And don't tell us it was a seismic study because the houses in this tract were all built after the building codes were amended to require houses to be braced for earthquake protection," Trish added.

Buchanan was quiet for a minute. Ellie and Trish couldn't tell if he was annoyed or taken aback because they'd both chimed in.

"Photos," he said. "I was looking for photos of Clarke Mobley. There's not one displayed on any of the walls, on bedside tables, or anywhere else. It makes me wonder how you felt about your late husband," he said tentatively.

"I hated him."

"Mrs. Mobley, Michaels, whatever... I want to remind you that you don't have to talk to me. But I can obtain a search warrant."

"I'm aware of that," Ellie said. "When my husband walked out on our daughter and me, it upset me to see his photos hanging on the hallway wall."

"She should have hanged *him*," Trish said.

"You're not helping," Bunny said quietly.

"After our daughter, Antonia, moved to the dorms on campus, the house felt particularly empty. I rearranged some of the furniture. And I removed Clarke's pictures."

"Did you destroy them?"

"If only," Trish said. "She brought me a box of them and asked me to keep the photos for Antonia."

"And you did that?" the detective asked.

"No, I took them out back and burned them," Trish said. "Just kidding. I was this close to taking a laundry marker and drawing mustaches and beards on all of them when my own husband walked into the room and suggested that he store the box of photos in his workshop until Antonia was back in town and could pick them up."

"I see."

"Does that satisfy you?" Bunny asked the man.

"Of course. I've been unable to get a 'read' on how Ms. Michaels or her neighbor felt about Clarke Mobley. That's all."

"Maybe that's because *I* don't know how I felt about him," Ellie said. "One minute I hate him for ruining my life, and Toni's, and the next minute I miss him. I despise what he did to us, and I hate that it all had to be so public. He'd already left us and moved in with Bambi. If he wanted to die in the nude, why couldn't he do it on her turf? The bastard." She hesitated a moment. "Sorry, Bunny," she said.

"I miss him on garbage day," Trish admitted. "He always brought our trash cans up from the curb when he brought his back to the garage."

"Would you like to see the photos?" Ellie asked. "I could call Harvey Grover and have him bring the box over."

"No. It's enough to know you didn't trash them. I'm sorry I've taken up your time again this morning."

He showed himself out the door.

And why not? Ellie thought. *He's here often enough.*

Trish moved the curtain aside and watched as the detective walked back to his car. "At least he was careful walking out," she said. "All spring flowers present and accounted for."

"Ladies, don't buy that 'country-gentleman-aw-shucks act," Bunny said. "He's trying his best to get one of you to incriminate the other. Ellie, you remind Antonia to talk to no one without counsel present."

"WHAT DO YOU suppose happened in Bunny's life?" Ellie asked.

"Beats me," Trish said. "What are you thinking?"

"Sometimes she relaxes and seems just like one of us," Ellie said. "But other times she's one tough cookie."

"Has anyone ever tasted a 'tough cookie'?"

"I'm serious," Ellie said. "I know we live in a relatively small area, but I'll bet that woman attorney commands respect statewide. When Bunny walks into a room, I swear people want to 'drop, cover, and roll.'"

"If I were guessing, I'd say she got steam-rolled once too often by men in her profession," Trish said. "And, when she got up off the ground, she swore that would *never* happen again."

"Could be. She's definitely the opposite of her sister Bambi..."

"...who could beat any man to the floor."

"Trish!"

ROD NELSON ARRIVED for work half an hour early on the first sunny Saturday in months. Santos was working on the side of the main building, unloading bags of potting soil. Rod pitched in to help.

When Ellie arrived the two were talking, laughing and tossing the heavy bags onto a flat-bed wagon to be pulled around to the side of the nursery where they had created a display area that made the bags of soil much more visible for garden shoppers.

"I don't know where you found this guy, El, but he knows how to work," Santos said.

"We hire only the best," she said.

Ellie wanted Rod to familiarize himself with the display areas of plants and how each group of annuals was priced. Two hours later she looked out the window and saw Rod helping a woman customer select a climbing rose bush. Within a few minutes, Ellie saw her new weekend hire walking toward the sales office, carrying a decorative trellis in one hand and pulling the tub with the rosebush in a wagon behind him. The woman was smiling and talking to him. He had an easy manner and looked like he'd been serving customers at Gardens and Greens for years.

Later in the day, Santos approached Ellie with an idea. If he and Rod squeezed in the work between their other tasks, would she mind if they distributed the cedar mulch that had been mis-delivered so it would spruce up the entrance to the nursery and make the area around the sales office look tidier?

"Did you explain the mulch situation to Rod?" Ellie asked.

"No," Santos said. "I thought the situation with the mulch might be private. Family stuff."

"Thanks for your concern," Ellie said. "But I think he needs to know in case a customer makes a comment.

Most people in the valley heard the news reports that morning."

"Right," Santos said. He hunched his shoulders and looked uncomfortable.

"I'm not sure I can tell him without tears," Ellie confessed.

"I'll talk to him," Santos said.

"Thanks. I also don't want him to freak if Detective Buchanan keeps rolling in here at all hours of the day."

"They're still working on the case?" Santos asked.

"Um hum. Every time I turn around the good detective shows up on my front porch at home. It's like having my very own Columbo. 'Just one more question, ma'am.'"

BY LATE SUNDAY afternoon, the nursery yard had been transformed into a pleasant display area, showing examples of the various uses for bark mulch in yards in the community. Instead of sitting in wooden trays, the dark green plastic containers of annuals now appeared to be growing from well-tended beds surrounded by mulch. As each container was sold, the men moved another plastic pot into its place. The walkway from the side driveway had potted geraniums and alyssum "growing" from mulch borders on each side. And the entire outdoor area had the clean, crisp smell of live plants mingled with that of cedar.

And, somehow, the men had managed to handle questions and serve the customers while freshening the landscape at the nursery. Ellie also noticed that the sometimes-shy Santos had followed Rod's lead and begun visiting with customers and carrying their purchases for them as they moved toward the cash register. Ellie heard him visiting in both Spanish and English with a young couple as he helped them pick out flowers to plant around the front porch of their home.

Had Santos been intimidated by Clarke before? she wondered.

The sprinklers somehow got moved from area to area at the same time the two men were serving customers who were eager to usher in a new growing season. She overheard Rod explaining to one woman how to modify the soil to change a hydrangea from pink to blue and watched as he showed another customer how to prune a rosebush above a shoot with five leaves.

Trish called late that afternoon to check on Ellie, who had reported that business at the nursery was picking up.

"New Guy Rod and Santos clicked immediately," Ellie reported. "They got more done in one day than Clarke ever did in a week. I think I can do this."

"Of course, you can do this."

"I know *you* believed that all along, but I had my doubts. Today, for the first time since Clarke left, I believe I can be the sole owner and manager at Gardens and Greens."

"How's that feel?"

"Like a million dollars," she said. "And that's a good thing because we need to make up for the sales we lost while we were closed down the week after Clarke's death. Although last weekend's sales were way above usual."

AFTER THE GATES were locked at the nursery, Ellie headed toward home. She was feeling happy, but exhausted. The Civic seemed to steer itself into the drive-up window at McDonald's. She ordered a chicken wrap for herself and a McFish sandwich for Felix.

The two of them were now stretched out on the couch, ignoring all earlier rules about not eating in the living room.

"If that's a telemarketer..." Ellie said as she eased herself off the couch when the phone rang. She recognized Toni's voice instantly.

"I'd have called earlier, Mom, but I went to a fraternity party with Mike."

"Mike?"

"We're in Sociology 101 together this term. The prof takes a smoke break half way through the class. Mike and I used that time to get acquainted. Mike's great. He grew up in Idaho, in a big family."

"I like his name."

"Mike? Mom, are you OK?"

"Isn't that my line?" Ellie asked. "I'm glad you called. I wanted to tell you that I filed the paperwork for my name change on Friday. I want to make sure you're OK—what with your dad gone and all."

"I've come around on that," Toni said. "It's kind of your business, isn't it?"

"I'm glad you feel that way. In a few weeks, I'll be Ms. Michaels."

"Mom!"

"BUNNY! WE WEREN'T expecting you," Ellie said.

She showed the attorney into the living room.

"Is Buchanan here?"

"No. Is he supposed to be here?" Ellie asked.

"You said 'we' and you mentioned the other day that the man visits often. Anyway, more often than you'd like."

"The 'we' is my friend Trish," Ellie said. "She's in the bathroom. She'll be right out."

"I've got news that I want to share with you two before I'm obligated to share it with the detectives conducting the investigation into your late husband's demise."

"Does 'demise' mean 'got what he had coming?'" Trish asked as she came into the room.

Ellie motioned for the two women to sit down. "What's up? Do I want to hear this?" she asked.

"In this case, I think you may," Bunny Maguire said in her courtroom voice.

"Spill."

"We now know why Clarke was back in Oregon during the time that Bambi reported him missing."

"How did *we* find out?" Trish asked.

"I threatened Bambi, but that needs to stay between us."

"You did *what*?" Ellie asked. "You threatened your own sister?"

"You may have noticed that Bambi and I are on separate career paths. When I was a sophomore in college, she was waiting tables at Red Robin. When I was studying for the Oregon bar exam later, Bambi shot up her own career ladder and was serving drinks at Hooters."

"We all have our own paths," Ellie said quietly.

"Good one," Bunny said, but Ellie suspected she didn't mean it. "Let's just say that Bambi's early career path gives me leverage now."

"How *did* you get Bambi to spill the beans?" Trish asked.

"Buds, not beans," the attorney said. "I threatened to cut off Bambi's trust fund payments until she leveled with the police. My law office oversees those funds."

"Sounds effective," Trish said.

"Brace yourselves," Bunny said. "It seems that one Clarke E. Mobley was in Oregon to check on the current cost of marijuana plants. He was trying to figure out how to cut costs by purchasing marijuana in Oregon and shipping it across state lines to Colorado, where retail prices on plants are higher due to limited stock."

"That's super illegal, isn't it?" Trish asked.

191

"It's a federal offense if you're caught. Two to fifteen years depending on the circumstances and the perp's past record." Bunny said.

"Did Bambi have any other details?" Trish asked.

"Only that pot inventory was larger in Oregon than Colorado at the time. Acreage in southern Oregon had shifted from pear trees to grapevines and wineries, and then to marijuana fields. With weather inversions, I've been told, you can smell the Oregon pot as you drive down Interstate 5."

"He was knowingly going to commit a felony?" Ellie asked quietly.

"Apparently without batting an eye," Bunny said. "Ethically, I'm required to share this information with Detective Buchanan, who has an open case. And I will," Bunny said.

She hesitated. "Off the record," Bunny continued, "I wouldn't share it with your daughter. It wouldn't serve any purpose but to further damage her father's image in her mind."

"Agreed," Ellie said quietly.

"Do you think this will make any difference in Buchanan's investigation?" Trish asked.

"Not officially. However, it can't help but taint the detective's view of the deceased."

"Again?" Trish asked.

"Buchanan will see one Clarke Mobley for the sleaze the man is."

"Was," Ellie said.

ELLIE HAD BEEN WORKING up her courage to ask Rod if he knew how Steve Evans lost his wife.

"I do, but I thought you weren't interested," Rod said when she finally inquired.

"Never mind."

Rod walked off to help a woman with one child in a stroller and another two trailing behind her.

When would this woman possibly have time to plant flowers and water them, Ellie wondered.

A WEEK LATER Rod passed Ellie coming out of the sales office at the nursery.

"Cancer," he said.

"What?"

"Steve and the boys lost Kara to cancer. She beat it once, but it returned in a more aggressive stage."

"How terrible."

"They had about six months after the diagnosis. Steve and the boys used every minute of it to be with her. In some strange way, since she was fighting a losing battle, it might have been a blessing that it progressed at that speed. Carter and Kent—their twin sons—would probably have delayed starting college otherwise."

"It's all so sad."

"Why'd you want to know?" Rod asked.

"Just curious."

"This is the Twenty-First Century. You could call the guy and ask to see his garden," Rod suggested. "Or his etchings."

Ellie picked up the wet sponge she'd been using to clean a ceramic pot and threw it at him.

"Employee abuse!" he called as he ducked the missile and went back to work.

"I GOT A TEXT from Toni this morning," Ellie said.

"She must be speaking to you again."

"Well, through cyber-space anyway. She got her winter term grade report and she had all A's and one B."

"That's incredible," Trish said. "With everything she's been through, I would have said a 2.0 GPA was a miracle."

"I think she used studying to block out some of the trauma of Clarke's death."

"Smart girl we raised," Trish said. "Can I tell Harvey?"

"Absolutely."

"I haven't heard much about Harvey's garden this year."

"You know better than most, El. It's a little early to plant yet," Trish said. "But, he's out there every day doing some tilling, turning up the ground..."

"I figured as much."

"He doesn't seem to have the same enthusiasm as past years. He's strained his shoulder some way or another. I labeled it 'old age' and he got grumpy." Trish hesitated, then corrected herself. "Grumpier."

"Be kind," Ellie said. "Retirement is supposed to be quite an adjustment."

"You're right, of course. But, he's also so absent minded. He's apparently lost the near new Pendleton shirt he got a couple of months ago. He's driven off to see if maybe he left it at the library."

"Working in the garden is probably good for him," Ellie said.

"Yeah. But, maybe you could remind him that most locals plant too much zucchini each summer? It'd be a public service announcement for him and the rest of the neighbors."

"Ain't it the truth. I'll see what I can do. Harv and I don't talk that often."

"IT'S ALMOST LIKE summer out there," Trish called to Harvey as she came in the door from her shift at the boutique.

"Don't get too used to it," he responded. "We always have a couple of days of false spring."

"I picked up some steaks at the grocery store. I could ask Ellie over for dinner if your shoulder feels good enough to grill them."

"Would you stop with the shoulder! It's fine."

"Yeah. That's why you were rubbing it when I came in just now."

15

It was 6:45 a.m. when Ellie approached the sales office at Gardens and Greens. She was earlier than usual arriving at work, and she could see two people inside. She took a few more steps before she could see clearly who was there.

Santos and Roamer were each holding a cup of coffee, but neither of them seemed to be talking. Was this a morning routine or did the two just happen to connect today?

Ellie opened the door to the office and Roamer started to rise.

"No need to get up," she told him. "It's super cold out there. I could use a cup of that coffee. Do you mind if I join you?"

Roamer looked uneasy.

"It's OK," Santos said. "This is the lady who owns the nursery."

"Know that," Roamer said. "Mrs. Mobley."

"And, you are?" Ellie asked.

"Just Bob."

"Welcome, Just Bob."

The man smiled a toothless grin and took another sip of his coffee.

"Hope you don't mind," Santos said. "We got a late frost last night and I thought I'd let our friend here warm up. It must have been bitter cold last night."

"Of course."

There was an awkward silence while Ellie took off her coat and hung it up. She poured herself a cup of coffee and walked over to the counter.

"Ma'am," the guest said. "Ma'am, I want to thank you for leaving that shed door open on winter nights."

"Must be my absent-mindedness," she said.

"Right," Santos and Bob said at the same time.

They sat in awkward silence sipping coffee.

"Bob," Ellie started. "Were you here the morning all the police cars came?"

"Fire truck too," he said.

"My husband died here that night."

"Not a good night, Ma'am."

"So, you were here that night?"

"I didn't hurt anybody," he said and started to stand.

"Of course you didn't. I don't think that at all. We know that you guard the plants at night," Ellie said. She was making this up as she went, but she wanted to make the man feel at ease.

"I scare the deer at night," he said. He made a loud sound that caught Ellie off guard. It sounded like the sound track from an old movie about cowboys and Indians.

Santos rose and topped off the coffee cups for all three of them while Ellie caught her breath.

"Careful, that'll be hot again," he told Bob.

"Bob, were you scared that night?" Ellie asked.

"Bob isn't scared," he said.

Ellie didn't miss that he talked about himself in the third person. She'd known other mentally challenged people who did the same thing.

"The girl was scared, but not Bob," he continued.

"There was a girl here?" Ellie asked.

"Right here. In this room."

"Had you ever seen her before?" Ellie pulled a photo of Toni from the plastic sleeve in her wallet. It showed Toni standing in her soccer uniform, posing with her foot on a soccer ball. "Is this the girl?"

"No. The girl is short."

"Was her hair like mine?" Ellie asked.

"No. Her hair is yellow."

199

"What happened to the girl?" Santos chimed in.

"The car came and took her away."

"Do you remember anything else about that night?" Ellie asked.

"Bob needs to go," he said. He put his coffee cup in the sink and pulled a black hat with ear flaps out from under his ragged jacket.

"New cap?" Santos asked.

"Bob doesn't steal."

"We know that," Ellie said. "Absolutely not. You watch over the nursery at night for us."

"It looks like it'll keep your ears warm," Santos said.

"Yes. It's your hat," Ellie said. Clarke had a similar hat, she remembered. He'd also paid way too much for a new winter jacket that she'd thought at the time was more suited for a snowy climate. Duh!

Bob thanked Santos for the coffee and went out the door.

"It's his hat now," Santos said with a chuckle. "I'd like to meet the man who's brave enough to take it from him."

"Well, that was interesting," Ellie said to Santos. "I've never spoken to the man in all these years."

"I've waved to him when I drive up to the job," Santos said, "but the guy makes himself pretty scarce. I've always wondered where he goes during the day."

"Me too."

"You didn't mind me helping him warm up this morning?"

"Of course not," Ellie said.

"WHO DID CLARKE know who had blonde hair?" Trish asked when Ellie repeated the conversation she'd had with Roamer.

"My first guess would be Bambi."

"Wouldn't Bambi be annoyed if she knew that Roamer described her three-hundred-dollar dye job as 'yellow' instead of 'shimmering platinum' or some other glitzy term?"

"It doesn't make sense that Bambi was out here. She can't be in Oregon and Colorado at the same time. The police reached her by phone in Colorado the night Clarke died."

"How do we know that? Maybe they called her cell phone?"

"I guess I just assumed they'd reached her at home."

"Detectives never assume," Trish chided.

"It was during the same stretch that the picture of their wedding arrived in my mailbox. That had a Colorado postmark. She can't have been in two states at the same time."

"I don't know, she's fast," Trish said.

"Yeah, yeah. Do I call Buchanan and tell him what Bob had to say?"

"Your call, as they say."

"I need to at least mention to him that Bob, alias Roamer, is at the nursery most nights."

"Where does Roamer go in the daytime?" Trish asked.

"From his appearance, I wouldn't be surprised if he has a hiding spot underground."

"Does it freak you out that he could have been watching both us *and* the police during those nights of surveillance?"

"I hadn't thought of that," Ellie said. "But now that you mention it, yeah, it does. Big time."

"I have something to ask you," Trish said quietly.

"Why so formal? Ask away."

"It's not formality. It's that I want your answer to be 'yes,'" Trish said. "Harvey's cousin Matt is going to be staying with us Friday through Sunday. Unfortunately, we already had plans for Saturday night and can't easily bring him along."

"I don't like where this is heading," Ellie said.

"He's a couple of years older than you are and he's a solid sort of guy. He's an accountant in Seattle."

"Please, no. Not another older single man. Has it occurred to you that these guys are single for a reason?"

"Matt's wife died," Trish said.

"Sorry. Let me correct that." Ellie said. "I'm sorry for his loss. But, that doesn't necessarily mean I want to be his next 'find.'"

"I'm not asking you to marry the guy. Harv and I need someone to entertain him for the early evening. Eat dinner. That's all. You both need to eat. Right?"

"True," Ellie said, "but there's no rule that says we can't each eat alone."

"Nonsense. Harv and I will even pick up the tab. We're in a bind here. We only see the guy every five years or so and we don't want to be rude."

"How do you know I won't be rude to him?" Ellie asked.

"Have I ever heard you be rude to anyone?"

"Well, not intentionally," Ellie admitted.

"If it makes it more comfortable for you, we can arrange it so you meet him at the restaurant."

"I suppose I..."

"Thanks. I knew you'd do it."

ELLIE COULDN'T predict the exact time she'd be able to get free at the nursery on Saturday to go home and change clothes before she was to meet Harvey's cousin.

She loaded her 'date clothes' into the car on Saturday morning. That way she could clean up at the nursery and change clothes. She sent word through Trish that she needed to meet Matt at the restaurant.

She'd borrowed a dress from Trish. She had the pair of heels that she'd worn for Toni's high school graduation dangling from her left hand.

"Big date?" Rod said as she walked across the nursery yard.

"Maybe. But, I'd rather you didn't mention it."

"Steve can take a good ribbing with the best of 'em."

"It's not Steve."

"Oops! Who then?"

"A widower from Seattle. He's related to Trish."

"Ahhh. We're branching out."

Ellie didn't respond.

"Why no divorced guys?"

"No comment."

She went out the office door toward the parking area. A minute later she returned for the paper bag full of dirty work clothes. *Was loss of memory related to divorce?* she wondered.

"IF I'M NOT PRYING..." Trish asked Ellie the next morning. "How was the big date?"

"You're prying." Ellie made a face at her.

"That bad?"

"Matt claims his wife died of a heart attack. But between you and me," Ellie said.

"Yes?"

"I think he bored her to death."

"Maybe I should remind Harv that you're a big girl and can get your own dates," Trish said.

"Hold on here. I thought I was doing you two a favor," Ellie said. "What happened to the schedule conflict you had with Matt's visit?"

"Now, don't be mad. It was Harvey's idea. We probably could have invited Matt to join us, but Harv thought it would be nice to give you and Matt a nice night out."

"Do you mind if I kill your husband?" Ellie asked.

"I wouldn't, if I were you. It might give Detective Buchanan more ammunition to use against you."

"Tell Harv that's the sole reason I'm sparing his life"

16

Harvey Grover backed his Jeep out of the driveway at his home and drove into Corvallis to the Emergency Care center. He didn't think seeing medical personnel would make his strained shoulder feel any better, but it might make Trish happy. She seemed convinced that he was neglecting his health

A young Physicians' Assistant who looked vaguely familiar entered the room and greeted him as she looked at his chart.

"You taking up boxing in your retirement, Mr. G?" she asked. "Have you got a good right hook that none of us knew about when we took your history class?"

Harvey looked at her again. She seemed familiar.

"My maiden name was Carrie Hunt. I took your US History class."

"Of course," he said. "It's always nice to see one of my students has succeeded later in life."

"Just don't ask me to name the US Presidents in order. "

"You're safe."

She rotated the shoulder slowly and carefully until he winced.

"Not good," she said.

"I think I may have hurt it gardening."

"A little early for gardening, isn't it?" she asked.

"The soil out at our place is pure clay. I've amended it through the years, but I still have to work it each spring. Maybe I overdid it this year."

"It was probably good for the soil, but not so wise for a shoulder that has possibly not had a good work out all winter."

Harvey silently wished that the next former student he ran into would be waiting tables or pumping gas somewhere. *And, please God, if I ever have an injury in a personal area, could you see to it that I get a male physician over fifty?*

"You say it came on suddenly?" the woman asked.

Harvey nodded.

"That's kind of the way shoulder injuries perform. They're not there one day and the next day they're in full pain mode."

She rotated the arm again, sending a shooting pain through his shoulder. "I'm going to prescribe a muscle relaxer for you to take at bedtime. Give me a call if the medication leaves you fuzzy or groggy and I can alter the prescription."

Harvey nodded. He didn't know if the pills would work, but he knew it would make Trish happy that he was tending to the injury.

He stopped by the pharmacy and then headed home.

"AM I THE ONLY one who feels like we're running in circles?"

"Isn't that what a circular floor plan is for?" Trish asked.

"Cute," Ellie said. "I'm serious. We make a suspect list, but it doesn't get us anywhere. Right?"

"Right," Trish repeated.

"We decide to stake out the nursery."

Trish nodded.

"We buy food. We drive your car so we won't be spotted. We hide the car in the trees. We almost get arrested."

"I know all that. Remember, I was there," Trish said. "Which reminds me..."

"Don't change the subject," Ellie said. "The night the police cancelled our stakeout, we stopped moving forward on figuring out why Clarke was back in Oregon. Unless, of course, the tale about purchasing marijuana in Oregon holds up. We're not even definite about whether he fell that night or if someone helped him hit the ground that hard."

"I see your point," Trish said.

"Had Bambi thrown him out?"

"I do know that theory doesn't work," Trish said.

"Why?"

"Bambi's the one who supposedly reported him missing."

"Oh, there's that... What can we do to get this investigation rolling?" Ellie asked.

"I've been thinking about all this. We need to interview the suspects," Trish said. "And, unless you want to travel to Colorado, I say we start with those who live in Oregon. Of course, they don't have to talk to us, but it'd take a lot of guts to tell the widow..."

"Bambi's the widow, not me," Ellie interrupted.

"...that they don't want to help put her mind at ease by finding out who killed her sweet, loving husband."

"Throwing up here."

BOTH WOMEN agreed that they had gotten off to a great start. "Very organized and professional," Ellie put in. But somewhere after arranging their list of suspects in alphabetical order, their investigation had fizzled.

"Maybe Buchanan's right," Trish said. "We suck as detectives."

"I hate that word," Ellie said.

"Buchanan?"

"No, the other one."

"We can leave it out of the interview questions," Trish promised.

"I don't think we're bad investigators. We just need to regroup. I say we look at our original list of suspects again."

"Minus Bambi," Trish said. "The cops cleared her."

"She's still at the top of *my* list. She's a 'lifer' as far as I'm concerned."

Trish ignored the comment. "I say we revamp the list. Add some, drop some."

"Like knitting?"

Trish ignored this second interruption also. "Then we put together a comprehensive list of questions based on the info that has surfaced." Trish blanched. "Sorry. Wrong word choice."

"No problem. If Clarke hadn't 'surfaced' that night, he'd have popped up somewhere else later. That's the problem with divorce. You think you've cleaned house, but you're never completely rid of the garbage."

"Be careful. You're starting to sound like me," Trish said. "Remember, you're the sweet one."

"My mom probably wouldn't have let me play with you when I was a kid," Ellie admitted.

Trish opened the laptop computer, ready to write some possible interview questions for the suspects on their updated list.

"Do you think people are going to let us waltz into their living rooms and quiz them about their potential ties to a murder victim?"

"*Potential ties*? See? You're sounding more like a detective every day," Trish said. "I say, let's write the questions, then do a practice interview to get the bugs out."

"Sure. Right. Once we're more at ease, we ask potential killers by for tea and grill 'em."

"Of course not. We can be subtle."

"Do we stick to our written questions or do we dig deeper after a suspect's initial responses?" Ellie asked.

"Play it by ear," Trish said.

"Let me verify something. So, after days and days of planning, we've decided to play it by ear?"

"Sounds like us, doesn't it?" Trish asked.

"It'd be nice if we could do a practice interview. But I repeat myself."

"Harv!"

"What about him?" Ellie asked.

"We'll use him for practice. But first we need to sequence the questions and practice taking notes and asking impromptu follow-up questions. Plus, we need to decide which one of us is the 'heavy.'"

"You're suggesting we do 'good cop/bad cop?'" Ellie asked. "Who's who?"

"Do you have to ask?"

Good cop Ellie didn't answer.

212

17

Trish, Harvey and Ellie were visiting in the Grover's family room after another one of Harvey's grilling successes. This time he'd barbecued chicken which he served with his secret-recipe for potato salad and a store-bought pie that Trish contributed. Ellie had brought a cold vegetable platter, but the chicken got cooked through in less time than Harvey had predicted, and her healthy contribution was set aside while they dug into the main meal. Dessert was on the kitchen counter.

The home phone sounded, and Trish picked it up and stepped out of the room so that Harvey, Ellie and Mary could continue visiting. She assumed she was about to meet another telemarketer and was ready with a glib reply. Instead, she heard the familiar voice of Detective Buchanan.

"Do you work twenty-four hours a day, or does it just seem like that?" Trish asked.

"Seems like that to me some days too," he said.

"Any chance your neighbor, the one with the killer cat, is there? I was supposed to purchase something for the Assistant Chief's retirement luncheon, and I forgot. I'm responsible for buying a group gift—something that can be planted in the yard of the new house that Ace and his wife have purchased for their retirement."

"Cute idea."

"Not if you don't know anything about plants," he said. "And not if you're supposed to produce said gift tomorrow morning."

"Oops!"

"I'm hoping that I can stop by Gardens and Greens on the way to work tomorrow morning. Purely business."

"I've got just the woman for you," Trish said as she carried the phone into the living room and handed it to Ellie.

"Buchanan," she whispered to Ellie.

Ellie made a face.

Buchanan repeated the details of his predicament a second time.

"You won't believe this..." Ellie started.

"I usually don't."

"...but I have three potted Olympiad roses at my house across the street at this very minute."

"You're kidding."

214

"No. I brought them home about six weeks ago to place under the back porch at my place where they wouldn't get caught in that late frost. The bushes are healthy—and ready to find a new home. All three are Olympiads and they do well in this climate. Olympiads are hybrid tea roses with a compact, velvety red bloom. Can you swing by the Grover's place in, say, half an hour?"

"I'm on my way. Someone else is supposed to be getting the garden furniture. The guys collected $75 for this part of the gift. Will that cover it?"

"Easily."

Ellie handed the phone back to Trish. "Well, that was stranger than fiction," she said.

"What did he want?" Harvey asked.

"You won't believe this. He's coming past here to buy some rosebushes I have at the house. Tonight."

THE GREAT ROSEBUSH transaction completed, Detective Buchanan walked Ellie back to the Grovers' house across the street and down the block. Ellie had resisted questioning him about what police policy was for transporting rosebushes behind the "fencing" separating the front seat of a police squad car from the backseats.

Harvey was watering the front lawn and Trish was sitting on the porch pretending to read a magazine. He walked over, turned off the water, and met Ellie and the detective in the driveway where Harv's Jeep was parked.

"Your rig?" the detective asked.

"Yes. I've had that Jeep since my last year in college," Harvey said. "That vehicle and I've decided to grow old together."

"That's not a vehicle," Ellie said. "That's a member of the family."

"I haven't seen one of these for a long time," Buchanan added. He leaned down to look inside. He walked around the car like someone inspecting a vehicle on a new car lot. A low whistle came out of his mouth. "That's some Jeep," he said appreciatively.

Before any of them knew it, Buchanan was down on the driveway peering under the back of the vehicle. Then, he was standing again, doing everything short of kicking the tires.

"Those mega-tires must cost a pretty penny," he told Harvey.

"More than I like to admit," Harvey said, stepping back a foot or two.

Trish noticed Harvey's discomfort, but the others continued to look at the Jeep, its restored paint gleaming in the partial light of early evening.

"If I'm not being nosy, what does one of those tires run you? And, where do you even find them in this town?"

"I'd tell you, but I'd have to kill you," Harv said jokingly. He knew Trish would probably kill *him* if she knew what he'd paid last time he'd replaced all four tires at once.

The detective was now looking at the undercarriage. "You take this baby out in the back country much?" he asked.

"Nope," Harvey said simply. Trish wondered why Harv wasn't talking up the car as he usually did to admirers.

Buchanan was now squatted down looking from the back tire, down the length of the car.

"Thinking of buying one?" Harv asked.

"No. Just admiring this one," Buchanan said.

Harvey looked the detective squarely in the eye. "Is there anything else you want to know?" he asked as the man ran his finger over the near-new tread of the back, left tire.

"Not particularly. Why do you ask?"

"I know you were out here once checking on the tire tread on Trish and Ellie's cars. It made me think you might be checking this one."

"Should I be?" Buchanan asked.

Harvey looked stricken. "I think we'd better all step inside," he said. "There may even be some leftover dessert."

Harvey led the way and the other three followed. Neither Trish nor Ellie knew what was going on, but they were afraid to look at either Buchanan or Harvey.

The detective spoke first as they sat down around the dining room table. "Do I need to apologize?" he asked. "I needed to check the tires on the women's cars to see if they matched a print left at the nursery the night

Clarke Mobley died. I could tell from across the street that your Jeep tires aren't even close to a match on the lead I was chasing at the time."

"You don't need to apologize," Harvey said. "I was the one who jumped to the conclusion that you were checking out the Jeep tires because..." Harvey hesitated. He took two deep breaths and cleared his throat. "...because that Jeep and I were at the nursery the night Clarke was killed."

"And?" the detective asked.

"We probably need to talk," Harv said.

Ed Buchanan noted that it was the first time he'd ever witnessed both Trish Grover and her neighbor Ellie speechless.

"You're up," he said to Harvey.

"I'VE BEEN living with some information for a couple of months now," Harvey said. "This isn't a case of 'the coverup is worse than the crime.' I didn't cover anything. None of you ever asked me any questions."

"If you have helpful information, sir, why didn't you volunteer it earlier?" Buchanan asked. "Where were *you* on the night of Clarke Mobley's death?"

"I attended a lecture at the university."

"What time did the lecture conclude?" Buchanan asked

"Just after ten p.m."

"You've got some time that's not accounted for, buster," Trish put in.

Ellie shushed her. Buchanan showed some interest in the conversation for the first time.

"Let him talk," the detective said. "As you ladies undoubtedly know, sometimes detectives learn more by listening than talking."

"Point taken," Trish said.

"It looks like the three of us are prepared to sit back and listen," Trish told Harvey. She glanced at the other two, who each nodded agreement.

"I was driving back home on the main highway, right past the nursery. And when I drove past, I thought I saw a light on in the sales office at Gardens and Greens."

"That would be unusual," Ellie said.

"I thought so too. I turned the car around and went back." He glanced toward the detective. "Frankly, I was afraid that these two were there, working late at night on straightening out the business records that Clarke left in a mess. Plus, Trish had told me that someone in Colorado had reported Clarke missing."

"And?"

"Something wasn't right. Even if it was Clarke, he had no business being there after the divorce. So, I made a U-turn and went back to the nursery. The only vehicles that were parked there were the nursery trucks. That seemed strange too—if there was someone in the office."

"Don't stop," Trish said. "We're all dying to hear this."

219

"I opened the door as quietly as I could, and I saw a young woman sitting on the bench along the side wall of the office."

"Please, say it wasn't Antonia," Ellie said.

"No. It was a young woman I'd never seen before. She could have been anywhere from high school to college age. There were tears running down her face and she pulled her ripped blouse toward her chin to cover herself as I stepped inside."

Buchanan noticed that Harvey was struggling with each word.

"Let's take a break," he said. "It will let you get your thoughts together."

The men stood up and stretched their legs.

Trish returned to the kitchen and served herself another piece of pie.

"GO AHEAD, when you're ready," the detective told Harvey after they returned to the table.

"You can imagine what was going through my head. The girl looked about the same age as Toni. My mind was flipping between trying to comfort her and being afraid that I'd be accused of having assaulted her—or whatever had happened to her."

"Of course," Buchanan said.

"About that time, Clarke staggered out of the bathroom at the back of the office. He was stinking drunk. Anyway, that was my best guess. It was a cold night and he was naked. He smelled like a brewery."

Ellie paled.

Harvey hesitated.

"It's very noble of you to want to confess, sir," Buchanan told him. "But, we both know that these two are involved up to their eyebrows in either killing or arranging to have Clarke Mobley killed."

"What if I could prove that I was at Gardens and Greens nursery that night?" Harvey asked.

"I understand your motivation," the detective said. "Even I've grown fond of these two over the past few months. But, how can you prove beyond a reasonable doubt that you were at the nursery?"

"Would a witness help?" Harvey asked.

"Possibly" the detective said. He took out a notebook and pen. "OK. I've got all the time in the world. Let's hear the rest of your story."

"You have to keep in mind that Clarke and I had been good friends at one time," Harvey said.

"What changed that?" Buchanan asked.

"First, he let his drinking get out of control. And then he started 'chasing skirt.' I lost all respect for him."

"And, you didn't tell me?" Trish asked.

"Was that Detective Trish or Wife Trish asking?" Buchanan inquired.

"Oops!"

"Go on, please," Buchanan said to Harvey.

"I took off my shirt and handed it to the girl to cover herself. I gathered up Clarke's clothes from around the room and shoved them toward him. He took them and stood there smirking. I yelled at him to get the H out of the office and off the property."

"Did he?"

"He took a swing toward me. I side-stepped, and he clipped me on the shoulder." Harvey hesitated. "I tried to shove him out of the office, but Clarke was a lot stronger than I am."

"And?"

"He stumbled around, dropped his clothes, and found his boots and put those on. Then he gathered up his clothes from around the floor and took off across the front nursery yard. He was half running and half stumbling."

"Clarke was running?" Ellie asked.

"As much as he could in his condition. Once he got past the light reflected from the office windows, I couldn't see which direction he went and, frankly, I didn't care."

"Go on," the detective said.

"I'd solved one problem, but then I was worrying about being alone with the girl. What if she'd had something to drink and got confused and thought I had harmed her in some way. I was a wreck. Nothing like this had ever happened to me before."

"Take a deep breath if you need to," the detective said.

"No need. I'm fine. I asked her how she got to the nursery because I didn't see any cars. She said she'd been at a pub where she'd had a drink and the man offered to take her home. He was driving a truck and said he needed to stop to use the bathroom at the nursery he owned..."

"Owned, my foot!" Ellie said.

The detective signaled her to stay silent.

"The girl said she believed him because his truck had an advertisement for the nursery on the doors. She left her own car at the parking lot at the pub. She thought Clarke was being protective when he suggested she come into the office to wait for him instead of sitting in a dark parking lot. Once they got inside, she said, 'things got ugly.'"

"And?" Trish asked.

"I asked her why she didn't call for help, either her folks or the police. She said she'd misplaced her cell phone somewhere between leaving home for the bar and arriving at the nursery. For all I know, she could have had a lot to drink also, but she wasn't incoherent or anything like that."

"Do you think she was old enough to drink?" Buchanan asked.

"I really don't know. As I get older, I can't estimate the age of young women as well as I could when I was teaching. But I know she couldn't have been much older than Toni."

'You mentioned Toni earlier," Buchanan said.

"That was part of my dilemma," Clarke said. "I think I'd have handled this a lot differently if I hadn't been trying to spare Toni from finding out that the Dad she loves—loved—wasn't the man she thought he was."

"So, what did you do?"

"I handed the girl my cell phone and asked her to call her parents. I told her to be sure to tell them that I would stay with her until they arrived. And, that I was NOT the man who assaulted her."

"I understand your hesitation to have Antonia see that side of her father, but why didn't you tell me about the encounter when you got home from the lecture that night? Or even the next day?" Trish asked.

"I thought I'd taken care of things the best I could," Harvey said. "Then the next morning you got a call from Santos saying that Clarke was dead in the nursery yard. I didn't know if you or anyone else would believe me. I didn't know the girl's name. And I didn't think to ask her parents their names. I had no way to prove why I was at the nursery that late at night."

Trish started to speak.

"Pardon me," Buchanan interrupted. "Do you still have the same cell phone, Mr. Grover?"

Harvey pulled an old-style flip phone out of his pants pocket.

"Do you mind if I take this with me?"

Harvey looked confused. "Me or the phone?" he asked.

"The phone," the detective said. "Before I leave tonight, I'll write a receipt for you so you'll have proof that I left with it."

"Sure. I seldom use the thing," he said. "But, what good will that do?"

"If we're lucky and, as you say, you haven't made many other calls since that night, it will contain a record of the phone number that the young woman dialed from the nursery."

"After all this time?" Ellie asked.

Detective Buchanan nodded.

"I never thought of that," Harvey said.

"If you've used the phone frequently, we'll have to rely on more sophisticated technology to dig deeper and recover that number. It's a little more complicated on one of these old flip phones. But that technology is out there and available to us."

"Thank God."

"Once we've traced that phone call, I'd like to assign someone from the police department to do the follow-up investigation with the girl and her family."

"Am I under arrest?" Harvey asked.

"Not yet. But until further notice, you are not to leave your residence or surrounding yard. I'm asking my two 'associates' here to monitor that you are abiding by that order. I'll be checking in with them frequently during the time that police officials are making inquiries."

"Of course."

"One other question," Buchanan said.

"Colombo," Trish and Ellie said in unison.

Buchanan frowned at them. "Again. What stopped you from coming forward?" he asked Harvey.

"Trish and I don't have children of our own. I've loved watching Antonia grow up." A tear rolled down Harvey's face and he hesitated before going on.

"Are you OK?" Trish asked.

Harvey ignored the question.

"Plus, by evening the day after I threw Clarke out of the office, the TV news anchors were reporting the 'grisly murder' of a man who had been smothered beneath bark mulch in the nursery he once owned. Because of the state of the body, they reported that police were checking on the whereabouts of known sex offenders. I was damned if I reported it, and damned if I didn't."

"Oh, Gawd," Trish said. "You've carried that fear all this time."

"I didn't have any choice. If I spoke up and said I'd been at the nursery that night, Antonia would have had her faith in another father figure dashed. If the abused girl's family couldn't be found, who was going to believe my only involvement was to throw Clarke out of his old business building? And it never occurred to me to take down the license plate on her folks' car."

"I know it was dark, but what did you notice about their car?" Buchanan asked.

"It was an older sedan. Possibly black or dark blue. Probably a Ford. Maybe ten to twelve years old."

"Think back. What else did you notice about it?"

"The upholstery in the front seat was torn. That showed when they opened the passenger door."

"Close your eyes a minute and think about the car some more," the detective ordered. "Concentrate."

"Nothing," Harvey said.

"Don't rush it. We'll step into the living room for a minute and you just concentrate on that scene and the car."

THE WOMEN WERE quiet. Trish was holding her breath, and Ellie chewing the fingernails on her right hand.

Buchanan was scanning the notes he had taken while talking with Harvey earlier.

"I've got it!" Harvey shouted. "I remember! Their car had one of those odd, undersized spare tires on the front passenger side. I was trying to remember which year car manufacturers started putting those in the trunk instead of a full-size spare."

Buchanan grinned for the first time since he had arrived. "Bingo! That's what I was looking for early on in this investigation. We've got a photo down at the office that I'll bet will match the tread on that mini-spare tire. It left an imprint in the mud at the nursery that night."

Harvey sighed heavily.

"Get some sleep," the detective told him. "I'll be in touch. If things fall into place as I suspect they will, you'll still face some charges. No promises at this point, but I doubt murder will be one of them."

18

As Buchanan pulled away from the curb in front of Harvey and Trish Grover's house, he could see the couple and their friend Ellie Michaels sitting in the dining room. He wished he could have hidden under that table to hear the conversation. The earlier confession had thrown him for a loop.

Harvey Grover was one of a kind, he thought. *The guy was a loyal neighbor. You didn't see that often during police investigations. People would sell out their own family members. Would Harvey Grover concoct this story to protect the victim's wife? Possibly,* Buchanan thought.

"Hell, Ellie Mobley-Michaels wasn't even on the police suspect list at this point," he said aloud. "But her daughter was. Would Harvey Grover admit to being at a murder scene to protect Antonia Mobley?" he asked himself.

Grover had better hope that the police could recover the number he claimed the young assault victim called that night, Buchanan thought.

If there even was a teenage girl. Or was Harvey Grover loyal enough to his wife's best friend to have whacked her louse of an ex-husband himself?

Information about the case and tonight's confession ricocheted about the detective's head. *Was Clarke Mobley conniving enough to have kept a key to the nursery after the divorce? And if so, were the keys to the trucks with the nursery logo on their doors available once the office door was unlocked?*

And as cold as it was, why hadn't a coat, gloves, or a hat been recovered during the search of the grounds. Investigators had found men's pants, a shirt, socks and underwear. That was it. Why wasn't the victim wearing warmer clothes in either Colorado or Oregon in early spring?

The case had legs, Buchanan thought. The minute they had chased down one theory and eliminated it, another would jump to the surface. *Was the crime Grover was copping to truly committed by Harvey Grover? Or was Mobley killed by someone else who had no business being at Gardens and Greens that night?*

BUCHANAN STARTED the following morning by thumbing through the stack of mail that had accumulated on his desk.

The City College brochure was there. No surprise. It arrived four times a year. He flipped through the pages and found that the campus was offering an introductory class in private investigation next quarter. He was aware that the college offered two or three law enforcement courses a term. Rookie cops saved a lot of tuition money by picking up those credits locally.

That course catalog worried him, though. If he'd been on the mailing list for the class descriptions, Trish Grover and Ellie Mobley-Michaels were too.

He acted instinctively. He picked up the phone and called to check in with Harvey Grover. While he was on the phone, he gave Grover permission to go as far as the mailbox in front of his home to retrieve the college publication—and throw it in the trash.

Buchanan would have to take his chances that Ellie Michaels tossed her class catalog along with the junk mail. His plan was to discourage—not encourage—the two amateur detectives he'd talked with the night before.

Buchanan had twinges of guilt about what might have been roughly called mail-tampering.

He'd soothe his conscience when this case was over by offering the women a tour of the downtown jail—in hopes that they'd realize neither one of them should continue in the criminal investigation business. One could always hope.

"HI, I WASN'T expecting you," Ellie said.

Trish rolled her eyes and came in the front door of her friend's house. She plopped down on the couch in the living room.

"Harvey is driving me nuts. I may be the one the police have to take into custody if Harv's on informal house arrest much longer."

"Sorry."

"I'm the one being penalized here. Thank you, Detective Edward Buchanan. Thanks so much."

"It can't be *that* bad," Ellie said. "How long has it been?"

"Two days, thirteen hours, and eighteen minutes."

"But, who's counting," Ellie said quietly. "Aren't there any projects he can do out in the garage?"

"He's washed both cars—daily—and he's now moving on to the garage. That's why I'm over here. He's adding shelving to the garage wall. That's the one on the other side of the dining room."

"Sounds productive."

"Sound is right. Pound, pound, swear. Pound, pound, cuss..."

"Well, you can always help me. I've decided to re-decorate Clarke's former study. I always wondered why the man even needed a 'study.' His laptop and printer were at the nursery."

Ellie handed Trish the spin chart of paint chips. "Would choosing pink come across as vindictive?" she asked.

"No, but if you did it the same color as the living room and exchanged the door for double French doors, it would add some light in here," Trish said.

"You've been watching too much HGTV," Ellie said.

"Not me. Harvey. House arrest has broadened his viewing habits."

19

The Grovers had a light dinner together and then waited nervously for Detective Ed Buchanan to arrive to talk with Harvey. Ellie and Trish had agreed earlier in the day that "house arrest" couldn't go on indefinitely for Harvey. If for no other reason than that it was driving Trish nuts! She had phoned Ellie the minute she heard that the detective was returning this evening and invited her to join them.

"Doesn't that man ever sleep?" Ellie asked.

"Doesn't appear to," Trish said. "Could you please walk down to our place and be here with us?"

"Of course."

For thirty minutes, the three of them sat in the Grovers' living room straining to discuss anything but Harvey's fate.

Trish knocked a glass of water over on the end table when she leaped up to look out the window and see if an approaching driver planned to stop.

"False alarm," she said as she sat back down again near where Harvey was cleaning up the spill.

There was a knock on the door five minutes later. "How did he do that?" Trish asked. "Did you hear anyone drive up?"

"Does it matter? He's here now," Harvey said. "Take a deep breath. Here we go," he said as he opened the door. "Nice to see you," he said to Buchanan as though they had been expecting him for Super Bowl Sunday.

"And, you," the detective replied briefly.

Trish rose and ushered the man to a chair. Ellie nodded and tried to make herself invisible.

"We're missing someone," Buchanan said. "Isn't your attorney going to be here?"

"I decided against it," Harvey said. "Trish thinks I'm nuts, but I want to hear the charges before I hire an attorney."

"Stupid," Trish said quietly.

"It would have been interesting for each of you to hear the lengthy discussions—plural—that we in the Detectives' Office have had with the District Attorney this past week."

None of them spoke.

"So much for ice breakers," Buchanan said. "Let me get right to the point. We were able to recover the phone number you claimed to have dialed that night at the nursery, Mr. Grover."

"And?"

"The three family members—the girl, her father and mother—agreed to come to the police department to be interviewed. I'll make this short. They corroborated your story down to the last detail."

There was an audible sigh in the room.

"While you had reason to regret that you hadn't gotten the license plate information from the car, they regretted that they hadn't gotten your name or address so they could thank you properly."

"No need," Harvey said.

"After several hours of discussion with the District Attorney over the past two days, we determined which charges will be filed against you under Oregon state statutes."

Harvey swallowed audibly.

"Let's start with those that we eliminated," Buchanan said. "I'll review those one at a time."

He cleared his throat.

"Based upon the information from the autopsy, we do not believe you are guilty of the crime of murder. Nor manslaughter."

The other three sighed in relief.

"The victim's injuries are indicative of someone who has suffered a fatal fall. And by checking delivery dates and times, we have determined beyond a reasonable doubt that the mulch covering the victim was not there while you were present at the scene. The parents of the young victim of sexual assault verified that you left the nursery at the same time they did."

The detective cleared his throat and continued. "Neither are you being charged with assault and battery. We believe you actually prevented that crime from occurring along with a possible rape of the teenage victim."

Trish reached to put her arm around Harvey.

"A charge of burglary won't stand up because it doesn't appear that any property was taken. Likewise, breaking and entering won't stick because the door to the office at the nursery was already open when you arrived."

The three listeners leaned forward, still waiting to hear which charges *would* be filed.

"Failure to report a crime in progress doesn't stand up. While we do encourage citizens to do their civic duty, there is no *requirement* that they do so. You are also not what the state deems a 'mandatory reporter,' and, thus, required to report abuse of a minor. In any case, the victim whom you prevented from further injury was forty-three days past her eighteenth birthday."

"We threw the idea of theft against the wall, but that didn't stick because *you* threw Mr. Mobley's clothes toward him as he left the office rather than taking them into your possession. The girl confirmed that," he added. "We determined earlier through DNA testing that those clothes did, indeed, belong to the victim."

Harvey squirmed in his chair but remained silent. Trish reached across and patted his knee.

"Charges of armed robbery don't hold up, either," Buchanan said. "According to our information, you were neither armed nor, it follows, carrying a concealed weapon."

He looked at each of the listeners individually, moving from right to left.

"Harvey William Grover, I am arresting you on the charges of 'failure to provide information in a timely manner to police' and 'trespassing' on real property that did not belong to you. You have the right to remain silent. Anything you say can and will be used against you in a court of law."

Harvey stammered, and Buchanan noted that never before had he seen Trish Grover nor Ellie Mobley— correction, Michaels—speechless.

"If you cannot afford an attorney, one will be appointed for you," he continued. "I can take you into custody now or, in my best judgment, place you under house arrest and order you to report to the police station at ten o'clock five days from now. That would be at 10 a.m. Friday. I am requiring you to notify me by 4 p.m. Wednesday if you wish to have an attorney appointed for you."

He finished speaking and the room was quiet.

Harvey slowly shook his head in disbelief.

Ellie and Trish hugged each other.

"I see this as both good and bad news," Buchanan said.

"It all sounded like good news to me," Harvey said.

The women nodded.

"What frightens me about the outcome of this," the detective said, "is that it frees up time for these two ladies to hone their investigative skills."

"I hadn't thought of that," Harvey said.

"So, before I leave tonight, I'd like to review Oregon State Statute 162.247, interfering with an official police investigation, with these two."

Both Ellie and Trish looked stunned.

"Then, folks, if you don't mind," Buchanan said, "I'm going to be on my way. It's been a long day for all of us." They all agreed.

"Oh, Mr. Grover," Buchanan said. "I recovered a shirt you gave to the assault victim. It's at my office."

He was almost out the door when he turned with one more comment. "You need to know, ladies, that the penalty for interfering with a police investigation could far exceed the sixty hours of community service I expect the judge to sentence Harvey Grover to complete."

20

"Hey, El," Trish said into the phone. "You do realize that Clarke caused his own death, don't you?"

"How do you figure?"

"Listen carefully. And, follow me here," Trish said. "Even I'll admit that this theory is a little convoluted."

"I'm listening," Ellie said.

"When Clarke ordered the *cedar* mulch--that's 'cedar' emphasized in case you missed it—he was intentionally vague so the company would send *you* the invoice. And, he hoped, you'd pay it without realizing it wasn't intended to be delivered at Gardens and Greens."

"I believe that."

"That *triggered*—and I like that word—the events that led to his death."

"Trish, that's a little far-fetched, isn't it?"

241

"Not if you remember that he ordered the bark mulch that smothered him," Trish said. "And, not if you think about it after a couple glasses of wine."

"Change of topic," Ellie announced. "I had a surprise phone call this morning."

"Toni?"

"No, but Toni's coming around. We both know that she's worshiped Harvey since she was a little girl."

"It's mutual. I remember when Harv called to me to look out the front window as Toni and her prom date left your house. 'Our little girl's all grown up,' he said. I've told that story a hundred times."

"Toni didn't like hearing what Harvey had seen at the nursery late that night," Ellie said, "but she believed every word of it."

"So, who called this morning?"

"Bunny Maguire."

"The Hare called?" Trish asked. "Why?"

"Our girl Bunny has an ethical streak. It probably goes with being an attorney."

"And she said?"

"She wanted me to know that she is helping Bambi with Clarke's estate."

"We could have guessed that."

"And when they were reviewing some paperwork, they discovered that Clarke never changed the beneficiaries on his life insurance policies."

"Policies, plural?"

242

"The primary insurance policy names me as the beneficiary," Ellie said. "And there's a smaller policy that I remember him buying that was supposed to cover Toni's college costs if he wasn't around to help with that."

"Hold on," Trish said. "Had he paid the premiums all these years?"

"The larger policy was paid in full about ten years ago, according to Ms. Maguire, now known as Attorney Extraordinaire. And I remember that the college plan was paid in full five or six years after he bought it. The total of the two—cashed out—should be enough to pay off the house and make some improvements at the nursery. And, of course, see Toni through college and then some."

"Unbelievable!"

"So, I am inviting you, Trish Grover, out to dinner with me to celebrate. And, for the record, I'm thinking a grade up from Wendy's or Taco Bell."

"I'm thinking filet mignon."

"Bunco!"

End Note

Bambi called Ellie in Oregon to say that she couldn't possibly make the funeral arrangements for Clarke in Colorado.

"I'm just too distraught," she explained. "There's no way I could entertain the guests from Oregon as well as the multitude of friends that Clarke and I have in Colorado."

Ellie Michaels waited silently to see what Bambi would say next.

"Clarke was so gregarious, you know, that everyone he met here just fell in love with him. It was one of the things we had in common. Neither of us has ever known a stranger."

Ellie bit her tongue. "Is there any other reason for preferring that the memorial service be in Oregon?" she asked.

There was a long hesitation.

"Can I be frank?" Bambi asked. "I don't want to be known as a widow. My sis says a widow can't date for an entire year."

Ellie stayed silent.

"You and I could save ourselves a lot of money by not transporting Clarke's body to Colorado and..."

Ellie could tell that the woman was building her case.

"And," Bambi repeated, "you and 'little Antonia' wouldn't have to travel. Our Antonia wouldn't need to

244

miss her school classes. Her well-being and education were so important to Clarke."

"I'll get back to you," Ellie said and hung up. She was afraid if she opened her mouth that she'd lose control. Frankly, she wanted to be a stranger to the woman. And, there was no way in hell that she was sharing Antonia with Bambi. They'd shared one too many family members already.

In the end, Ellie, Antonia, and Trish made the arrangements in Oregon for a small but tasteful service to honor Clarke Mobley. Ellie promised to mail his ashes to Colorado with hopes that Bambi would at some point confuse them with those she was removing from used ash trays.

"Ashes to ashes and butts to butts," Trish said under her breath.

Chairs for ten to twelve guests were placed outside the orchid house at the nursery. Santos, Rod, and Harvey re-arranged some of the potted plants to provide a proper yet cheerful atmosphere. Ellie thought the three men, Antonia, Trish, Bambi, Bunny and she would be the only mourners. To her surprise, she saw Detective Edward Buchanan standing respectfully to the left of the gathering.

Roamer stood a few steps back on the other side. It was a warm evening, but, out of respect, Roamer, alias "just Bob," had changed into his new leather coat. The one with the fleece collar.

Everyone except Trish wondered how a single sprinkler head—the one beneath Bambi's folding chair—

malfunctioned and soaked the Colorado widow as the words to the final hymn filled the air.

"As usual, there is a great woman behind every idiot." John Lennon

Acknowledgements

Thanks to new readers and past followers of A Designer Mystery series who indulged my whim to take a break and create a new cast of characters for *Can I Kill Him Now?* The story line in this quirky mystery hangs on the camaraderie between two friends. I have friends and family members of my own to thank for their support. I thank you all.

Special thanks to my sister Margie Smoak who reads early drafts and gives me quick and blunt reviews. (This time she lobbied for character Bunny to have a larger role and a better wardrobe.) My sister Nancy Sturm provided gardening tips and first-hand knowledge of plants in Oregon. Her country gardens are living proof of her expertise.

Additional thanks to my walking partners Kim Sass and Tess who offer encouragement at every step, and to friend Karen Shafer for wisdom and laughter.

My long-time "conspirator in crime" Kitty Buchner has been promoted to co-publisher, a title that offers little esteem and, alas, no paycheck, but tons of gratitude. Without her, there would be no quirky mysteries. She can spot a typo from across the room and has never met an errant adverb she didn't lobby to delete.

Author

Kathleen Hering lives in Albany, Oregon, where she writes at the wooden desk behind the kitchen and enjoys watching the deer and squirrels through the window.

She started writing fiction after retiring from public schools where she was employed as a journalism teacher, a middle school principal and later as a school district personnel director. She is married to journalist and radio and TV news commentator Hasso Hering. They spend their leisure time riding a tandem bicycle, rowing a red canoe, and enjoying their grandchildren—not necessarily in that order.

Readers can contact Kathleen Hering at
designermysteries@gmail.com.

Other Books by Kathleen Hering

Designer Mystery Series

Hammered, Nailed and Screwed

Oregon interior decorator Laura Howard is receiving messages from her husband on her telephone answering machine. It's his voice all right. But his ashes are in the urn on Laura's fireplace mantel...

Ripped, Stripped and Flipped

Laura Howard does not intend to keep the gift someone left for her in the yard of the 19th Century Italianate house she's restoring. And, detectives don't plan to close their investigation until they find out who delivered the gift, a corpse wrapped in newly poured concrete.

Studs, Tools and Fools

Interior Decorator Laura Howard had her life planned down to the last piece of designer drapery fabric. That was before she made that ill-fated trip downtown and landed smack dab in the middle of a bank heist. Now instead of juggling fabric swatches and designing dream kitchens, she's dodging threats and dealing with a cop a day at the Portland Police Bureau.